On Grizzly Mountain

David Hoffman

On Grizzly Mountain

Cover art by Stock Schlueter

Paperback ISBN: 978-0-9997645-4-1

To Robert Works Fuller

Chapter 1

Sasha Simonov headed north along the very edge of Western civilization. Appearing through the mist, the Golden Gate Bridge connected his past and future. The city he left behind remained shrouded in fog. He breathed a long sigh of relief as he drove through the toll booth without stopping. The free direction seemed a good omen. On the other side of the bridge, the sun had broken through. Sailboats dotted the bay like sugar candies. The golden hills around Sausalito beckoned him. For the first time in a month, he felt a surge of optimism. The pain of loss and rejection had finally begun to recede.

He had left it all: his house, his wife, his car and his job. He was no longer Professor Simonov, associate professor of Russian studies. He had bet it all on becoming a back-to-the-land itinerant pot grower, an outlaw. His former student, Carl, offered to set him up. When Carl wrote to say he'd be leaving for some time and would rent him his house, Sasha jumped at the chance. The sheer audacity of his decision was liberating. He had craved getting out of his comfort zone. He knew absolutely nothing about living in the country, as equipped to live on the land as a Neanderthal would be in Manhattan. Now, here he was driving up 101, surrounded by late model BMW's and Mercedes in a gun-metal grey 1962 Chevy pickup he had bought from a friend of a friend who knew someone in the San Francisco Mime Troupe who was moving in the other direction. The bed of his truck was filled with manure, covered in a green tarp. In the rearview mirror, he could see steam blowing from its edges.

That very morning, having transferred the title at the DMV and passing his California driver's test, he had backed his truck, which he had affectionately named "Tuffy," to the loading ramp at the rear of the elephant house at the San Francisco Zoo and proceeded to shovel a half ton of pachyderm shit, which he intended to turn into gold. He hoped this alchemy of transformation would also be his own.

Carl had told him to pick up some burlap coffee bean bags for collecting "cow pies," whatever the fuck they were, which he found at the Graffeo Café in North Beach. He fell in love with San Francisco, hanging out in Ferlinghetti's City Lights bookstore, ground zero for the beat poets he had once wanted to be. But books had become an albatross for him. He gave away a couple thousand of them before leaving his university life, an act at once self-flagellating and cathartic. He had defined himself by these tomes. His collection, he now admitted, was wholly pretentious. The more he shed of his old self, the freer and more authentic he believed he'd become.

He turned on the 8-track tape player that sat on the seat next to him. The faux leather was frayed and torn with some of its stuffing coming out. Listening to the Grateful Dead made him want to get stoned, but he decided to wait until the heavy traffic died down. There was something about riding up high in the cab of a pickup that ratcheted up his testosterone. The truck seemed to bounce on its springs as if he were riding a horse. He was having his California moment and it felt good. He wished he had Darlene sitting next to him, but there would be other Darlenes, he was sure.

An hour later, the traffic had begun to thin. Long rows of grape vines turning red stretched to the horizon on either side of the highway. There were wisps of mistletoe hanging from tan oaks that grew on the bald hills. Passing Healdsburg, he lit up a joint he had rolled before he left. He noticed there were more pickup trucks and old Volkswagens now than new model cars. Tuffy seemed at home here.

He had little idea what to expect when he got to Carl's, but the sense of adventure, of a new beginning, made his heart beat faster. By the time he finished his joint, he was alone on the two-lane road, not a car in sight. Time seemed to stop. He still had four hours or more ahead of him. He wondered whether he could last through a whole bag of M&Ms, if he let one after another of them melt in his mouth; but by the third one, he surrendered and chewed the rest.

Above the rumbling of the engine he heard crows cackling. He turned off the Dead and rolled down his window to listen. The air was fresh and crisp as the landscape gave way to larger trees and faster rivers. Two deer darted out from the side of the road. The vast empty spaces drew him in. He felt a lightness he had not experienced since the summers when he was a child.

Along the Eel River Canyon, somewhere between Laytonville and Leggett, three hours after crossing the Golden Gate Bridge, he pulled off the two-lane road to grab something to eat. The orange neon sign for the Howling Wolf Café said "open." A single car was parked outside. There were redwood trees, taller than any trees he'd ever seen, on either side of what looked like a broken-down motel. But stepping inside, he was astonished to find himself face-to-face with a fully grown African lion. Along the back wall of the café were booths you'd expect to find in any road-side restaurant, but they sat against large picture windows through which one could watch a veritable menagerie of large, exotic animals in a zoo attached to the rear of the cafe. The owner, a tough leathery-faced woman named Gretchen, explained that she had rescued all these animals, paying for their care by renting them out for television ads. Raised in zoos, they were quite tame, she assured him. In the early mornings, she even took her beloved Mercury Cougar on runs with her through the nearby hills, she told him. He tried to imagine what it would be like to come across them on their morning jog.

After a cheese burger and a milkshake, Sasha continued driving north, following the curves of the Eel River through untamed stretches of California's vast wilderness. He passed by the touristy "Drive Through Tree," a hollowed-out giant coastal redwood that, for a small fee, you could literally drive your car through. There was a long stretch of these ancient redwoods along either side of the narrow two-lane highway at a place called Richardson Grove. He leaned forward and strained his neck to see these largest living things on Earth.

4

Coming out on the other end, he passed an emporium of chainsaw-carved statues of bears, Indian totem poles and even Snow White and the Seven Dwarfs, and, finally, a sign for Garberville, five and a half miles ahead, it said. He got off there, gassed-up and, following Carl's instructions, turned onto the narrow Alderpoint Road and began circling higher and further from civilization than he had ever been before. Rolling grass-covered hills stretched to infinity. There were occasional cows grazing, but no fences and no sounds. Near the top of the hill he stopped and turned off the engine to take in the sublime stillness. He was enchanted by the buzzards that circled lazily above him. He experienced a religious epiphany. All that was seemed to lay before him, a God's eye view, and all was perfect and beautiful. He thought of Meister Eckhart's observation, "The eye by which I see God is the eye by which God sees me."

After about 15 miles, he descended to the tiny town of Alderpoint with its single post office, general store and a school that looked abandoned. He didn't stop, but continued another five miles, crossing a bridge over the Eel River, and turned right onto Wallace Ranch Road, a dirt lane that meandered through tall fir trees, ancient oaks, madrones and large open meadows. The road ended three miles ahead at a round wooden yurt with a large wrap-around deck next to a small pond, exactly as Carl had described it.

There was a blue pickup truck parked there, but no sign of life. He got out of Tuffy and petted the hood as if it were his horse. The vastness of this space filled him with awe. It was colder here. He could sense the coming of winter. Down the hill from where he stood, he noticed a thin line of smoke and he followed a path through a grove of madrone trees to its source. He came upon a circle of people seated on logs trimming pot, breaking down branches of cannabis with bulging colas at their ends. A yellow lab ran up to him, tail wagging. Sasha crouched down and held out his hand. "You must be Caliber, I bet." Two other dogs followed, a brown mutt and a grey Australian cattle dog who competed for pets.

Carl jumped to his feet when he saw him. "You made it!" he shouted and embraced him in a bear hug. "Let me introduce you to my friends."

Everyone was beaming, radiating the joy and excitement of a successful harvest. "Sasha, this is Kimmy, my ex-girlfriend," he said with a smile. Kimmy stood and hugged him.

"Do you remember me?" she asked. "I was in your Intro to Russian History class."

"How could I forget," said Sasha.

She had a cheerleader's body with long blond hair tied in a ponytail with a piece of twine. Carl had written Sasha that they had broken up. He was going off to Thailand by himself right after he sold his crop and he offered to rent Sasha his place. Kimmy, he wrote, would inherit their grow holes, but he would keep rights to the house, which he agreed to turn over to Sasha for sixty dollars a month.

"And this is Bruce. If you ever need anything, he's the man to ask." Bruce had unruly brown curly hair and a long, scruffy beard with specs of pot leaves clinging to it. His eyes were the grey of wolves', but his laugh was mirthful, like a child's. He was barefoot with strong sinewy arms and rough hands. He stayed seated, raised his arm above his head and shook Sasha's hand with a powerful grip. There was something feral about him. But his self-assurance softened his edges and his laugh was infectious. Sasha was immediately drawn to him. Kimmy sat down close to Bruce. It was obvious that he was her new man.

A woman about Sasha's height with short dark hair stood up and handed him a joint as thick as his thumb. Her eye contact was soft and warm, but intense, as if she were searching for anything untoward about him. He smiled back, openly, and took the joint from her hand. He inhaled deeply, the sweet pungent smell filling his lungs while he continued to hold her gaze. She had dark, mysterious eyes and long lashes. She could be Syrian or Palestinian, he thought. He felt the pot hit the back of his head right away and spread through every part of his body, inflating his senses. The warmth of the greeting and the hallucinatory high of the pot enveloped him with a feeling of belonging.

"I'm Miriam," she said, "but everyone calls me "Meer or Meera." Their eye contact didn't falter.

"I'm Alexander, but everyone calls me Sasha," he said, passing the joint back to her. With anyone else, such intense eye contact would be unnerving, but he felt the opposite. He felt an acceptance, a welcoming.

"Just call him Professor," quipped Carl.

"Not anymore," Sasha laughed.

Chapter 2

A light breeze blew wistfully through the leafy campus as Sasha Simonov, the precocious associate professor of modern Russian history, hurried along the uneven stone path late for his morning lecture on the Soviet period. He made it just in time, but out of breath. His heart beat fast. Nervous as usual, he studied the large hall filled with undergraduates, most of whom looked like they had stayed up all night.

The class was a popular one, largely because Professor Simonov was known to give easy grades. But they liked his wit and passion as well. There had been a few times, however, when his exuberance got the best of him and some of the boys in the back rows laughed derisively, making fun of him. The humiliation he felt then were wounds he still carried. But the mostly freshman and sophomore students, who hadn't yet attained the cynicism of upper classmen, genuinely appreciated how seriously he took his subject matter.

They were studying the origins of the Bolshevik Revolution. A black girl in the front row with an Afro twice the size of her head, raised her hand. "How come, if you hate the

Communists like you says, you get so excited 'bout them?"
The class broke out laughing.

A boy just behind her joined in, "Yeah, you're like roman-
ticizing them."

Sasha smiled. "First of all, what they pulled off was pretty
audacious, don't you think? I mean, they were a tiny group of
revolutionaries who managed to seize control of one of the
largest countries on earth. It's easy to demonize them, but I'd
rather get into their heads, try to understand what they believed
in, what made them think the way they did. If you can find
something to love in what you hate, you've got a better chance
to neutralize your enemies." For a generation convulsed by
culture wars and protest movements, Sasha's lectures seemed
more relevant than most.

It was his passion, more than the content of his lectures, that
taught his students that issues mattered and that a knowledge
of history was more valuable than any academic achievement
that might come with it. Professor Simonov made them grapple
with philosophical arguments that determined whether millions
would live or die. In posing these big moral questions he seemed
more in tune with the zeitgeist of this younger generation than
many of his older colleagues, several of whom looked down on
him. Indeed, he appeared to be not much older than the
undergraduates he taught. He was of medium height, had
short curly dark hair, wore John Lennon glasses and dressed in
blue jeans and running shoes. He was popular with the students
for having once recited a poem by Gary Snyder at one of the

campus sit-ins against the war, and had become a mentor to a small group of the more serious-minded political activists.

A few of his female students also took his wife Sarah's upper-level class on *The Second Sex*. They liked her, loved the readings she assigned, but some of them could be put off by what could seem like an overly academic approach to something so personal to them. The more radical feminists, though, adored her. They speculated endlessly about the relationship of the two young married professors who could hardly be more opposite. Where Sarah could be critical, dogmatic and ideological, Sasha thought ideological rigidity was the fountain of all evil. He was decidedly more of a humanist and far too humble to be dogmatic.

After Sasha's lecture, a knot of students lingered after class to engage him in discussion. Although he appeared shy at the lectern, even stuttering at times, in person he was warm and engaging. This day, after lecturing on Edmund Wilson's *To the Finland Station*, Sasha collected his notes, answered their questions and headed out into the sunlight of a beautiful blue-sky day with billowing cumulus clouds overhead. The nervousness he experienced earlier had left him and he felt buoyant and optimistic. The lecture had gone reasonably well, he thought. As he skipped down the steps to the quad on his way to the library, he heard Larry Kneeland's high-pitched voice. "Wait up, professor. Whoa, slow down."

Larry was Sasha's closest male friend. A professor of English literature, he had just attained tenure that year. Larry had honed a reputation as an extreme cynic, but that masked a very vulnerable, romantic nature. He was a few inches shorter than Sasha and had wiry red hair, pale blotchy skin and small rodent eyes. His brow had deep furrows across it. He walked with a slight limp. Known for making outrageously sexist and politically incorrect comments, he was a harmless provocateur. Sasha adored him. On Tuesdays and Thursdays, they worked out together at the gym and went on weekly hikes. They shared a love of John Coltrane. They also shared a love of women.

"Where you going so fast?" asked Larry.

"I was heading to the library, but I'd love to get a coffee. Wanna join me?"

"Sure. The Grind?"

Larry inclined his head. They veered off together towards the cafe. "How'd your class go this morning?" he asked.

"Pretty well," smiled Sasha. "I did *To the Finland Station*. I think even Lenin would've been proud. What's new with you, Larr?"

"You remember Carl Katz, that kid who hung the Resistance Week flag from Sieman's, the one who got kicked out and moved to California to grow weed?" asked Larry.

"The one with the dreads and the bad teeth?"

"Yup. Well, he came by to visit last night, was here for a friend's wedding. He brought me some of his crop, got me really fucked up," Larry looked around to make sure nobody could hear them. "I mean really fucked up! He's got some new way of growing the stuff," he explained, "something called sinsemilla, pot without seeds. They get rid of all the male plants and just grow females. The colas are like fucking Amazons.

11

You wouldn't believe the size of the buds. I've never seen anything like it. It's fucking amazing, like ten times stronger than that Michoacan grass we've been smoking. I had three hits and couldn't function."

He looked around them again. "Carl says the female plants keep putting out more and more resin trying to attract some male pollen. All their energy stays in the bud and doesn't get wasted on the seeds. I wish humans had the same philosophy. All that female energy turns it into a potent aphrodisiac. I got so horny I thought about having sex with our cocker spaniel, but then remembered Butch was a guy. Carl left me some. Stop by sometime and we can get wasted together."

"I will for sure. I need some more pot. If you see him again, ask if he'll sell me an ounce, will you, and I'll pay you back. How's Carl doing, by the way? I liked that kid. He had that beautiful hippy girlfriend who didn't wear shoes or bras, as I recall. I wonder if she went out there with him? How's he liking California?" Sasha asked.

"Loves it. He and that chick are living together growing organic vegetables. Sounded like Gilligan's Island. He's driving a brand new four-wheeler, too."

"Must be some damn good vegetables," laughed Sasha.

"No shit. When you try this stuff, you'll understand. You might want to quit this gig and follow him. I think he knows something we don't. Imagine, he's living in the mountains with his babe and only works half the year gardening. They're going to Thailand for the winter, he said. Told me I could come visit him," Larry went on.

"Maybe we both should quit," said Sasha. "Honestly, I'm getting tired of this routine. I feel like a hamster on a wheel. I'd love to get out of here, change my life. This teaching business is too damn safe. I envy that kid,"

"I'm too much of a pussy," said Larry. "I'm afraid I'd get busted and spend the rest of my life in prison getting butt-fucked by big muscled guys with tattoos."

They passed two girls in short skirts. "Nice ass," Larry remarked.

"Which one?" asked Sasha turning.

"The one on the left, in the denim."

They stopped near the cafe in the shade of a large syca-more tree to continue their conversation outside of earshot.

Sasha went on, "When I graduated high school I thought I wanted to be a poet. But I didn't have the balls. After college I went to grad school mostly to stay out of the draft and kind of just drifted into teaching history. I love the subject, but I feel like I'm living in a bubble. It's la la land here, not the real world. We lecture about people doing real things out there, but I feel like we're living in a dream world."

Larry smiled. "Maybe you're right. We should both just leave here together and grow pot out West. Marsha loves growing things. Would do her good."

They walked into the cafe and took seats under a poster of Bob Marley. The smell of coffee brewing was intoxicating. They sat on wooden chairs with orange cushions. They each looked around to see if any students they recognized or other professors were nearby. The café was largely empty. A skinny blond with a ponytail down to her waist walked over holding two pots of coffee. Sasha looked up. "Regular, please."

Larry thought for a moment, "I'll have some decaf." She poured them both. "Anything else?" They shook their heads.

They talked about the latest news from Southeast Asia. "Let's face it Larry, the Sixties are over and we lost."

Larry grimaced. "This country has more resiliency than a cockroach."

They talked for a while longer about Nixon, about metaphysics and back again to sex and pot. Then Larry said, "I've got to go, but I'll see you at the gym tomorrow?"

"For sure," said Sasha. "And bring some of that pot with you."

Larry paid. They parted with a wave. It felt awkward to Sasha to hug and worse to shake hands. Larry went back the way they came and Sasha hiked over to the gleaming new library, walked up the steps and through the large glass doors. At the entrance was a towering atrium that occasionally trapped errant pigeons. It was cool inside and quiet. Sasha loved the peace of it. He passed by the rows of card catalogues in their identical oak drawers and over to the Reserve desk. A woman with strawberry blond curls piled on top of her head turned as he approached and smiled at him. His heart fluttered for a second. She had large round green eyes and freckles. Her smile was like sunshine. She looked like the proverbial farmer's daughter. He was a little taken aback and he hesitated for a moment when she asked how she could help him.

"Hi. I'm Sasha Simonov, from the history department. I need to place a hold on a book for my class. Is this the right place?" He wanted her to know right off that he wasn't just another student.

She stuck out her hand unexpectedly. "Glad to meet you. I'm Darlene, Darlene Greene." She laughed as she said this, still smiling, revealing deep dimples.

"Was she flirting with me?" Sasha wondered, returning her smile. "Those dimples!" He stole a surreptitious glance at her body. He hated when he met a woman with a beautiful face, only to discover she had a body that didn't go with it. But this Darlene was beautiful from top to bottom. A sleeveless white blouse came off her shoulders and two breasts, round as snow globes, protruded from the top. He smiled extra hard now. He tried to remember why he was there.

"I wonder if I'm at the right desk. I need to place a hold on a book for one of my classes. It's by Arthur Koestler, *Darkness At Noon*."

Her eyes widened. "I've heard of that. What's it about?"

She's definitely flirting, thought Sasha. His heart beat faster. "It's about the Show Trials in Russia. It was written right after the Nazi-Soviet Pact when Stalin was purging the leaders of the revolution. It's the story of one of these leaders who was arrested and forced to confess to crimes he didn't commit."

Still smiling, her eyes squinted, thinking. "Forced how? Was he tortured?"

"No, not really, not physically. That's what the book's about. He knew he'd be shot, if he didn't confess and probably shot even if he did. But that wasn't the issue for him. The Communists—he was one of their leaders—believed so strongly in the rightness of their cause, that for them the end always justified the means, no matter how atrocious. He agreed to fall on his sword for the revolution."

She pondered this. "So, it was a moral question." She thought some more. "I guess if you feel that way, you can justify all kinds of crimes like Roskalnikov."

Sasha was taken aback hearing this. He hadn't expected this young woman to reference Dostoyevky. He got very excited. "That's it, that's exactly it. The only difference was that Roskalnikov believed in the individual and these guys believed they were on the side of history." He worried he was talking too much. "You should take my class. You get it! Are you a student?"

"I was," she smiled, but I graduated last year with a degree in anthropology. I'm not sure what I'm going to do now, but after sixteen years of school, this gig gives me a nice break."

Sasha could smell something delicious on her freckled skin as if she, herself, were ripe. His heart was racing now. He wasn't sure what he should do. Though he constantly fantasized seducing beautiful women, he had never seriously considered having an actual affair. But he now felt himself being irresistibly drawn to this strawberry blond librarian. His heart was throbbing out of control. He was sweating. Alarms were ringing and red lights flashing in his head. He told himself not to panic, not to make any hasty mistakes.

They went through the formalities of placing a hold on his book and then he heard himself ask her, "Would you like to get a coffee or something after work sometime?"

Darlene's face lit up. "I'd love that. I work till 5 each day. Come by and get me sometime."

"I will," said Sasha and he left, feeling like the character in *Darkness at Noon*, unsure what to do, but knowing that his fate awaited him.

Chapter 3

He was in his study at home when he heard the sound of laughter coming from the living room. He walked quietly down the stairs like a thief. It was Alice's voice he recognized. He liked Alice, liked her edgy, take-no-prisoners attitude and her robin-egg blue eyes. He couldn't tell how she felt about him, though he suspected she desired his wife.

The laughter was infectious. He could make out Carol Bennington's childlike giggle and stifled one of his own. It would be way uncool to be caught eavesdropping on a radical feminist consciousness-raising group, he knew. He had only wanted to slip into the kitchen for a bunch of cherries. He heard his wife Sarah say, "Go on, Alice. Go on. What happened next?"

He sat down on the step and listened. "It was like fucking 98 degrees outside," Alice recounted, "and I was up on the scaffolding with no shade. The other framers, all guys, started peeling off their T shirts, one after the other. When the guy next to me lifted his arms and took his off, I didn't stop to think. The whole front of my blue Patti Smith top was already soaked. I was dripping wet. So, I pulled it off. I hadn't even realized that I wasn't wearing a bra. When you're as flat chested as I am, you don't think such things."

There was a moment of silence in the room. Sasha could sense them holding their breaths, waiting to hear what came next. He imagined Alice taking off her blouse to show them. He remained motionless. The cherries could wait. Sarah, impatient as always, exhorted Alice to continue. "Oh my God! What happened?" He pictured Alice's blue eyes flirting with his wife, making her wait.

"It took a minute for it to register with the other carpenters," Alice continued. "It was already a stretch for them to have a real live girl on the job. They were on their best manners. Several of them laughed, a few even clapped, but I could see the others getting angry. They didn't like me being there at all, but this was too much. Frankie, the foreman, the guy I told you about with the mom-in-a-heart tattoo, unbuckled his carpenter belt and let it fall to the ground. Soon the others followed and I was left braless and alone two stories off the ground with a hammer in my hand."

Carol's roiling laugh broke over them in a cloudburst. They screamed with delight like a whole preschool class being tickled. When the laughter died down, Alice went on. "After a few minutes Frankie climbed up the scaffold, carefully avoided looking at me, and told me to go home for the day and not to come back without a top on. The rest of the men huddled around their pickup trucks, smoking, laughing, stealing glances. I climbed down and went home. I didn't know whether to feel

19

victorious or defeated. But when I told Carey about it, she had an idea. We found an American flag in the basement and cut and sewed it onto one of my bras. The next morning, I showed up with my red, white and blues under my shirt and when the men again took their shirts off, so did I. They didn't quite know how to react, but soon were hi-fiving me. Frankie was nowhere to be seen."

Sasha stood up. He didn't want to press his luck. He tiptoed down the stairs. The kaleidoscopic laughter hid the squeaking of his steps. But an old and uncomfortable memory intruded on his thoughts. The levity of female laughter turned in his head to sounds of angry arguments between his parents. He had sat on a similar flight of stairs as a young boy of six or seven, his forehead pressed against the wooden banister, listening as his father railed against his mother, first in English, but as their fighting inevitably escalated, in Russian. He had trouble understanding all of it. Too terrified of his father's alcoholic rage, he had sat frozen on the stairs hating himself for his impotence. He was his mother's son, but hadn't the courage to protect her.

Lightly sliding his fingers along the wallpaper like a blind man, Sasha slowly went down the stairs. He turned his mind back to the hysteria coming from the other side of the living room door, to Carol's irresistible Woody Woodpecker laugh and Alice's blue eyes. He tiptoed down the hallway and into the black and white Fifties style kitchen, its Formica counters littered with casserole dishes and a large glass bowl that still held the cherries he craved. Feeling like a thief, he tasted the remains of the potluck bonanza.

The crusty bottom of the tortilla casserole took the prize, he decided. There was something with marshmallows that looked more interesting than it tasted. Crumbs from a cherry pie was all that was left in one dish and the remains of a vegetable medley of some sort looked tired and unappetizing. He grabbed a half a brownie, took his bowl of cherries and started his retreat back upstairs to the safety of his study.

As he cautiously climbed the stairs, though, he became aware of a sour sense of alienation, of loneliness. Maybe it was the memory of his parents, he thought, or just being left out of all the fun. He wished he could be one of the girls. He always felt more comfortable around them than being with guys, he reflected. At parties he often gravitated to the kitchen enjoying the easy conversation of women. He'd do the dishes, an excuse to be there and a way to earn big Brownie points for being so politically correct. Sarah had trained him well. In general, he found men boring. Several of his friends had urged him to join their men's group, but the idea of sitting around with a bunch of hairy Neanderthals beating drums depressed him. He did host a group at his house on Wednesday evenings that was usually all male, but it was to discuss radical politics. The talk was all cerebral; and though they would sometimes focus their analysis on the need for men to be in touch with their feelings, that conversation, too, never ventured very far from the left side of their brains.

Alone in his office, he sank into a red leather recliner and looked at the photographs on the wall behind his reading lamp. A grainy black and white picture of a man with dark beady eyes, long unkempt hair and a drooping mustache was of his father. He was leading a donkey carrying a woman dressed in a hijab, his mother, and unseen underneath the folds of her robes, Sasha in utero, crossing the Hindu Kush, towering snow-covered mountains in the background. This was the family's founding myth, recited at every gathering: how Sasha's parents escaped from the Soviet Union ahead of advancing Nazi troops with the help of some Uyghur smugglers in the summer of 1941. Conceived in the small village of Orynin in Western Ukraine, Sasha had travelled across the whole of Central Asia and China before catching a freighter in Japanese-occupied Vladivostok for Australia and finally landing in New York two days before his birth, thereby automatically becoming an American citizen.

Sasha's father was a self-taught intellectual, an "auto-didact," as he liked to call himself, a brilliant polymath who spoke at least a dozen languages. His fluency in Turkic dialects earned him respect from his Uyghur guides and by the time he reached Vladivostok his command of Mandarin and Canton-ese had saved their lives several times. They were interred there by the Japanese, but he managed to talk his way out of that with the help of a generous bribe of hashish that had been hidden in a tunic covering his wife's pregnancy. Sasha liked to say that he came to his love of marijuana honestly.

Sasha's mother was also something of a linguist and an unrecognized scholar of Russian literature. She had passionate dreams to do something big in her life, but had never acted on them. Sasha often worried he was too much like her. He never took big risks, he realized. His mother was kind to him and patient, willing to spend endless hours helping him with his school assignments. But she was not an affectionate person and rarely held him. Whenever he kissed her, he'd feel her tense and pull away. He got her undivided attention and love, but not the kind he craved. Despite this, he was an optimistic person and emotionally self-sufficient, his optimism and sense of humor fed by a hyperactive imagination, vivid with color and sensuality.

He grew up poor, but well-educated, in Russian émigré neighborhoods of Brooklyn. His parents had little interest in conventional work or even the comforts it could buy. Baptized in the Russian Orthodox Church but committed atheists, they survived by giving foreign language lessons to the children of rich Russian émigrés, his father once teaching a Jewish kid his Bar Mitzvah Aliyah in Hebrew. His mother also gave lessons on the oboe, whose haunting sounds would fill their small basement apartment. He had no siblings. He spent a lot of time alone, though he made friends easily. He never played team sports, but was active in the theater and hung out with a bohemian crowd of budding intellectuals.

Chapter 4

That weekend, Sasha and Sarah had a couple from the university over for dinner.

"That was fun," he said, after they left.

"Yeah, I enjoyed it. They're really nice, though, I don't know how Karen can put up with those eyebrows. Men must think they're a sign of great intelligence, but it's simply a sign of bad grooming. Which reminds me, you're looking pretty scruffy yourself these days. You need a haircut," Sarah reflected.

"I do," he admitted.

Sarah filled one side of the sink with soapy water and began rinsing the plates in the other basin.

Hurrying over to her, Sasha said, "Here, let me do these. You cooked."

She shook her head, "No thanks. You never do them right. You can dry."

"We need a dishwasher," he said.

"I'm not going to spend all that money in a house we're renting. It makes no sense. We can get by this way just fine."

They were quiet for a few moments. Sarah put a hand on her waist, "I really need you to pay more attention around here, do your part," she said. "I can't believe you just spaced out the dinner tonight and left me with all the cooking."

She was right, he knew. "Hey, I'm really sorry. I apologized already. I won't let that happen again, promise."

Sarah wasn't done. "If it weren't for me, we wouldn't even have any friends. All our friends are people I've made an effort to get to know. The only real male friend you've got is Larry and you know I can't stand him, or Marsha, for that matter. Why don't you make friends with Ken? You two share a lot of interests. It would be good for you to have a friend who's a little older." She shook her head again. "Men have such problems being intimate."

Sasha frowned. He hated these discussions. "You're probably right," he admitted, hoping to end the conversation. "I like Ken. Good idea. I'll give him a call."

They finished the dishes in silence. Sarah wiped her hands on a dish towel and looked up at the clock over the fridge, frowning. "It's almost nine already. I still have a couple papers to read. I won't be long."

Sasha reached for her arm and pulled her towards him. "Look, hon, I'm sorry about tonight, about forgetting we had guests. I enjoyed listening to you tell about your dissertation. You were really on your game. I loved watching you. I'm sure someone's going to want to buy the movie rights when the book comes out."

Sarah laughed. He put his arms around her and held her. She didn't push him away. Before he let her go, he met her gaze and kissed her. It was a quick short kiss on the lips, not with any passion, but accepting it signaled enough forgiveness to make him think maybe there was some chance they'd make love that night. It had been eight days, he calculated. Sarah stepped back and retreated out of the kitchen and up the stairs to her study.

Sasha turned and went out through the screen door to the back yard. He wanted to get high. He knew Sarah didn't like him to smoke pot when they made love. She thought he used it as a crutch. But Sasha loved having sex when he was stoned. He loved to smoke at movies, too. It just amplified all the senses. Why did she care, if something made it more pleasurable for him? The real question was why didn't she get high. It pained him that she was so repressed, always needing to be in such control. *I could make her so much happier, if she let me,* he thought.

It had cooled considerably outside. Clouds moving across a moonless night revealed glimpses of stars. He went into the garage which held their bikes, some garden tools, garbage cans and boxes of their things piled in stacks along the back wall. He turned on the dim overhead light. There was an old sink that no longer worked and a medicine cabinet. Sasha walked over to it and pulled it out from the wall a few inches. Behind the cabinet, pushed up against the beams was a plastic bag with his stash. It was almost empty. There was a joint that had hardly been smoked and a pack of matches.

Sasha lit the joint and inhaled deeply. He thought about the pot that Larry told him about. He was anxious to try it. As the pot began to work its magic—he noticed the sense of time slowing and his attention lingering on his thoughts as if separate from him—he pictured the girl in the library with the green eyes and round breasts and how she smiled at him. He'd love to smoke pot with her, he thought. He imagined them passing a joint between them, perhaps in some seedy motel, and then his leaning towards her, kissing her, and cupping her breasts in his hands. He imagined her lying back and him unbuttoning her blouse. But then he forced himself to stop fantasizing. If he were to have any chance of making love with Sarah this night, he told himself, he'd need to stay connected to her. He did not want to be unfaithful to her, even in his head. He thought instead of all the things he loved about Sarah, her cute body, the sharpness of her mind, her independence. She was so self-contained, so impervious. The word stuck in his mind. He loved her for this strength, for her self-confidence; but it left him feeling unneeded. It had been a long time, he reflected, since she had shown any real desire for him.

He put the bag of pot back behind the cabinet, went into the house, and turned off all the lights downstairs. Sarah was still in her study. He went into the bathroom and brushed his teeth to keep her from smelling any pot on his breath. He usually could get away with stealing a few hits without her knowing, but he had to be careful. She'd be pissed if she caught him. He got in on his side of the bed with a copy of Shunryu Suzuki's *Zen Mind, Beginner's Mind*, which Larry had loaned him. He was searching for some more meaning in his life. He needed something new, something that would shake up the all too predictable life he was leading. The end of the war in Vietnam and the culture wars at home had left him feeling empty, as if a moral compass had lost its magnetic pull. He wondered if he should practice meditation. *Maybe I should try LSD,* he thought.

He waited for Sarah to finally come to bed. He closed his eyes and thought again of Darlene. Yes, he was sure that was her name. He felt his heart race. Then he thought of Alice and Sarah and imagined that somehow the chemistry of the three of them would ignite the passion that had seemed to steadily slip away from his marriage. It had been great when they first got together, but that unquenchable passion had been quenched, subsumed by the treadmill of their professional lives. In the split screen of his pot-infused mind, though, a voice told him the solution, if not the problem, lay with him. He should not depend on getting his happiness from Sarah. He had to find it himself. And he believed that if he did, it undoubtedly would make him more attractive to her.

Just as he was about to doze off, he felt Sarah slip in next to him. He had not even heard her walk in, though he had been listening for her. He opened his eyes and turned to face her. She was wearing the lace negligee he had bought her at Christmas and smelled of soap and body lotion. She smiled at him and he felt a rush of desire for her. How very easy it was for her to turn him on, he thought. He felt a slight resentment at the unequal power she held, but wanted her regardless. It had been several nights since he had stopped trying to initiate sex with her after a week of being rejected. He ought to reject her sometime, he knew, but he couldn't bear to wait so long again. It was humiliating to be turned down so often. But this was man's fate wasn't it, to always ask, leaving women with all the power? He had spent a lifetime being turned down by women, he reflected. He had made up his mind to stop asking and wait for her to. But now he felt Sarah's hand on his thigh and he knew his luck had changed.

He reached for her breast. She didn't try to stop him. He felt her nipple harden under his thumb. Her hand moved from his thigh to his penis, now swelling with desire. He wanted desperately to kiss her with their mouths open, tongue touching tongue, but he knew she hated that. She fondled his penis carefully like something delicate. He wanted her to be rougher, more aggressive. But he had learned the routine. He gently moved her legs apart. His left hand found the moist opening and he put his finger deep inside her. She sucked in her breath and then rolled on top of him, as she almost always did, grabbing his erect and obedient dick in her hand. He tried ever so stealthily to move down on her, but she wouldn't let him. When he stopped she went down on him, very briefly, then put him inside of her. They moved together in an ever more frantic rhythm until she let out a high-pitched squeal that seemed squeezed out of her as if she did not want anyone to hear it. A moment later he exploded with a muffled cry that gushed from his loins.

They lay silently next to each other on their backs. She leaned over and kissed him chastely with closed lips and smiled. Then she turned on her side facing away from him. Sasha lay there half in relief and half in despair. He knew she had given him all she was capable of, but he wanted so much more. If only they could talk about it, but every time he tried to bring up his desire to go down on her, she got angry and refused to discuss it. He felt powerless to change things and he hated himself for not being stronger. He was afraid of her, he knew, afraid to stand up for himself, to be true to himself, for fear she would take away the little that was left of their sex life. He rolled next to her and put his arm around her and then his mind turned to Darlene.

Chapter 5

Sasha felt oddly self-conscious as he got dressed in the men's locker room of the university gym. Everyone around him seemed part of the natural order of things. But Sasha never felt like he belonged. His purpose was minimal maintenance, keeping just fit enough to stay thin and burn off the excess calories from his indulgences. He put his things in the tall metal locker, snapped his combination lock, tied his high-top tennis shoes and went into the "factory" as he liked to think of it, a chrome palace of torture machines, walls of endless mirrors and body parts. It smelled of perspiration and rubber. To his right were the real men, muscle boys lifting free weights with the obligatory grunts of gladiators, biceps bulging under low-cut, sweat drenched sleeveless T shirts. He veered to the left by the front doors where a long line of stationary bikes and treadmill machines morphed infinitely inside a hall of mirrors. Larry was already mounted on one of the stair masters furthest from the entrance. Sasha got on the one next to him.

Larry, out of breath, greeted him, "How's it going, Sash?

"Good. What's new with you, Lar?"

"Carl's coming over later. I'll get you some of those nutritional supplements we talked about. I assume you still want them. Got any time after this to come by and try some?"

Sasha finally managed to program his machine to a reasonable rate and started his endless climb, like Sisyphus. "You tenured elites seem to have all the free time in the world. We proletarians have to actually work for a living. What time's he coming over? I can't go this morning. I'll need some time to finish reading the papers I blew off yesterday. But later. Sure. I'd love to."

"Call me when you're done, then," said Larry.

Sasha felt himself ease into a sustainable rhythm with the machine. "Hey, I'm loving that *Zen Mind* book you loaned me. It speaks to me. I need something to get me out of this endless routine. Life's starting to feel too much like this machine, stairs to nowhere. Anyway, I loved it, especially that part about 'the only way to control a cow is to give it a large green pasture.' I wish I could get Sarah to read it. How did you get into this? Do you meditate?"

Just then their conversation paused for a moment as a girl in grey spandex tights and long black hair walked through the front doors and signed in. Tall and thin, she had a dancer's body.

"8," said Larry.

"8.5" said Sasha.

"You always like those flat-chested model types, don't you?" noted Larry.

"Definitely!" answered Sasha. "I know you prefer the curvaceous species, but all that extra subcutaneous fat is vaguely repulsive to me."

"You're just repressed," said Larry.

Two more women came in. But they didn't rate a score. "Sarah would kill me if she ever heard how we talk," Sasha said.

"You're too pussy-whipped, man," replied Larry. "Sarah's got you on a tight leash. No green pasture for Alexander," he laughed.

"None at all. She's a total control freak. But it helps me understand the Stalinists I'm studying. They're convinced they know the truth and that it's their rightful place to keep the rest of us in line."

They didn't say anything for a couple minutes. Sasha was surprised by what he had just said. He knew it was true, though. She was always mad at him for one thing or another, much of it petty in his mind. It was only when others saw it, that he allowed himself to recognize it for what it was. Sasha spoke again, "So, where were we? Oh yes. I asked if you meditate?" asked Sasha.

"Marsha and I sit for a half hour every evening after dinner. It helps with digestion."

Two cute co-eds with identical blue shorts, white T shirts and peroxide blond hair walked up to the front desk.

"9 or 9.5," said Sasha.

"10, if you take them together," said Larry.

Sasha spent the rest of the day at a desk hidden away in the history stacks on the third floor of the library marking student papers. It was hard for him to concentrate. He badly wanted to see the blond librarian again, but his guilt felt like a noose tightening around his neck. He was the moth and she the flame. It was dangerous, he knew. But he had also fucked last night and he realized that he was sated enough to resist, at least for now. By day three or four, he might not be able to.

Around 2pm he was getting too hungry to stay put any longer. He walked down to the first floor and turned towards the front door without looking at the reserve desk. He hoped she would have seen him. It would be better, he thought, that he not appear too anxious. There was a pay phone by the men's room. He put a dime in and called Larry. "Hey, it's me. This a good time to come over?"

"Perfect! Carl's just leaving." Larry's voice sounded distorted. He seemed to struggle with every word. "Can you come now?" he droned. "I'll tell him to wait."

"Be right there."

Sasha pulled his bike from a rack beside the library and was at Larry's grey two story brick house two minutes later. A shiny new red Chevy Blazer was parked in the driveway. He left his bike leaning against a wall by the side of the house. There were raised beds of flowers and vegetables that stretched around to the back. He saw Marsha in a gardener's smock bent over one. She didn't see him. He walked around to the front, climbed the stone stairs and rang the bell. A moment later Larry appeared, his eyes red, pupils enlarged, looking slightly deranged.

"Come in," he said with a voice that tried to imitate some old horror movie.

Larry entered and walked back to the kitchen where Carl was sitting. The pungent smell of pot hung in the air. Carl turned and stood with a big smile on his face. His teeth were still badly in need of work, but he looked slim and vibrant, healthy and more muscular than Sasha remembered him. He held his arms open for a hug. Sasha obliged. The teacher-student relationship no longer applied. Sasha stepped back to look at him. He seemed somehow grown up, as if fully formed, comfortable in his skin. His long Rasta braids gave him a wild, untamed look. He was holding a fat joint in his hand. He held it out to him. "Want some, professor?"

Sasha took the joint between his thumb and forefinger and inhaled deeply. It tasted sour with resin and a slight taste of nectarine, he thought. "So, this is the stuff you're growing?"

Carl smiled. They sat down at a table made from old barn wood. The kitchen had a faux farmhouse look. Sasha didn't feel anything immediately from the pot. "It's good to see you, Carl," he said. "Larry was raving about your pot and about you." He looked over at Larry. "He does look pretty shit faced right now, doesn't he?" They all laughed. "So, you're living in California, living the farmer's life?"

"I am. Outlaw farmer. Grow all my own vegetables, all organic, and this sacred herb."

Sasha still didn't feel anything and took another hit. Carl's eye contact was a little intense, but Sasha met his gaze and didn't look away. "What's your situation, like where are you living, what kind of scene?"

Carl laughed again. He laughed a lot. "Right now, we're living in an old double trailer way up in the hills away from everything, me and Kimmy. You may remember her. We're building a house, a sixteen-foot yurt, but it's not finished yet. No electricity. It gets brutally hot, but there's a pond next to us where we go swimming all the time."

"Just the two of you?" Sasha asked.

"Yeah, and a dog, Caliber, an old yellow lab. It's totally beautiful. We're up a long dirt road. There're three other houses in our little community; but otherwise, no one's around for miles."

"Sounds like paradise. What's a typical day like?" asked Sasha.

"It depends what month. Right now it's super easy. All our plants have been sexed and are in the ground. I water the garden and pick yellow leaves off the pot plants, which will grow to twice my size. We probably spend more time with the vegetables now than we do with the weed. There's always things to do just to live out so far—water lines to fix, road repair, chopping wood, stuff like that. In the evening we read or play music." He paused, laughing to himself. "And fuck a lot. What else do you do when you're high all the time?"

Sasha considered that. Carl offered the joint again. Larry passed it on and Sasha took another hit. It tasted strong, but he still didn't feel anything, he told himself. Or did he? It felt like he had been there a long time, but realized he could only have just arrived. Now he was getting it. He looked at the sunlight streaming through the kitchen window, how it sparkled off the glasses sitting on a wooden shelf. He noticed little details, the freckles on Larry's arm, the rings at the end of Carl's dreadlocks. He started to feel giddy. *No wonder he laughs so much,* thought Sasha. Then he started to laugh himself, for no reason.

Larry smiled at him, "Nice, isn't it?"

"Yeah. Sweet," said Sasha. He noticed a slight buzz in his head. *Buzz,* he thought. *So that's why they call it a "buzz."* He was hyper aware of his thoughts. It was as if the witness in his consciousness and the voice of his thinking were separated somehow. Believing he was having some profound insight, he realized that the Self had these two distinct voices—the one, the witness, that was like neutral, a blank slate, and this other, that was an awareness of his perceptions, and maybe a third, his thoughts, in language, speaking to himself. But who originated these thoughts? Was it not him? Was it some inner wizard behind a veil, like the wizard of Oz? Was there a thought that came prior to its verbalization? Wasn't the thinking we did with language a representation of this prior, original thought? Like the map is different from the territory.

All of these thoughts passed in a moment while Sasha sucked on his fourth toke. As he passed the joint back to Carl, he thought that better be his last and maybe he had already smoked more than he should. He didn't want to get paranoid. He wanted to stay cool with Carl, normal. He had seen guys get way too stoned. He thought of that guy in the bowling alley who couldn't stop shaking his legs and everyone thought he was going to have a heart attack. He told himself not to worry like that. Fear like that can bring on a heart attack. You get what you fear. It was at that moment that Sasha spied the bag of cookies on the table. It was from Rita's Sweet Shop. He recognized it. A kind of coconut base with a chocolate frosting they called a Mexican macaroon.

Carl saw him staring, leering, at the bag and passed it to him. Sasha felt a real love for this guy. He was to be admired. He had cut his ties to the treadmill of expectations which society had foisted on him and was living in freedom. And sex with that girl without shoes or bras! *Oh my God*, thought Sasha. This Carl does know something we don't. *Larry and I are sitting here like we're bolted to the floor and this guy can just float above it all, or drive that new Blazer out there.* It surprised him to hear himself ask, "So, how much do you sell this stuff for? It's amazing."

Carl smiled, "Four hundred a pound."

"A pound?" Sasha laughed. "I've never seen a pound."

"You want to?" Carl reached an arm down next to him and lifted up a blue gym bag. He unzipped it and pulled out a plastic bag that was shrink wrapped, clinging tightly to marijuana buds the size of thumbs or bigger. "This is a quarter pound. He opened the gym bag. There were three more inside. He handed the bag to Sasha whose eyes widened at the sight of so much weed. "You'll notice there are no seeds. These are all seedless female plants, sinsemilla."

"Wow!" said Sasha. Larry was smiling like an imp, clearly too stoned to talk. "So, how much if I just wanna buy an ounce?"

"Oh, I'll just give it to you at the wholesale price, say 400 divided by 16, that would be just $25."

Sasha couldn't believe that Carl was able to do the math in his head as high as he must be. Sasha couldn't have. He reached for his wallet and took out a twenty and a five. "Here. I'd love some. This is like smoking LSD."

"Have you ever taken LSD, professor?" asked Carl.

"No, I haven't," said Sasha reaching for his second macaroon.

"You should, man," said Carl. "It'll open you up. It will reveal truths to you. You'll see the world as it more truly is. A lot of bullshit will just fall away."

Sasha smiled, nodded his head in agreement, feeling warm and happy. Very happy. Carl pushed a baggy filled with pot to Sasha. "Larry said you wanted some, so I already weighed this out for you, 28.35 grams." Carl stood up to leave. Larry and Sasha did, too. They all shook hands, then hugged. Carl turned to Sasha. "You should come visit sometime. Or come stay. It's a good life." He took out a paper and wrote down his address.

Chapter 6

The weather had turned blustery, threatening to storm. The color of the air grew dark and gusts of wind blew branches and leaves about. Sasha walked quickly past the library, hurrying to his little office in Gilman Hall. A girl with a long blond braid, black sweater, purple leggings and Birkenstocks walked briskly in front of him. He could hear her whistling to herself. *Yes,* he thought, placing a sex roulette bet on her being a fuckable candidate. He sped up to get a look at her from the front. She turned slightly at his approach.

"You," she said, lighting up.

"Uh, Darlene," said Sasha, taken by surprise. He slowed his pace to walk next to her. "I didn't recognize you right away with your hair down. I like it. Where you heading?"

"I've got to go home to feed my cat and get a bite to eat. Want to come along?"

His heart skipped a beat. He felt his temperature rise. He looked; there was no one around him. He meant to say that he had papers to grade, but instead said, "Sure."

"Where do you live?" he asked.

"I've got one half of a duplex on Grenada Street, off Oak. My roommate's in Chicago visiting her parents and I forgot to feed her cat this morning. What about you. It's Sasha, isn't it. Sasha Simonov?"

"Good memory. Yes. I was just heading to my office, but a walk sounds great, before it rains." They heard thunder in the distance. The light had turned a dusty yellow.

"Isn't it exciting," she said. "I love this weather. I hope it storms like mad. I'd love nothing better than to spend all afternoon in my bed curled up with a book."

"That sounds great." A clap of thunder, much closer. He got a better look now at her body. She was thinner than he remembered, long legged with a high, rounded butt like the black girls on the basketball team. She looked and walked like an athlete. He kept pace with her. "A book and a glass of wine or a joint." He commented, wanting to see how she'd react.

She laughed. "A joint would be better, but then I wouldn't be able to read." Now his heart was really racing. He had a joint from Carl's stash in a smell-proof plastic bag in his pocket. Should he bring that out now, he wondered, or was it too soon for that? He could deploy it, if the situation warranted.

"Did you play sports here?" he asked instead. "You walk like an athlete."

She smiled. "I played field hockey one semester but tore my meniscus cartilage. You?"

"I bike a lot. I played beatnik in college, not sports. I was mostly into poetry.

"That's so cool. You still write poetry?"

41

He looked down. "Not really. Not anymore. I gave that up when I went to graduate school. Had to make a living, I guess."

"Do you like it?"

"What?"

"Teaching."

"Yes, but no, not really. I do sometimes, but lately I just feel trapped, like I never really had a choice, though I obviously did. It just feels so safe. Being an associate professor is lots of work and little pay. You're under pressure to publish, tenure track and all, but it's kind of bullshit. If you stick it out long enough, though, you get to coast for the rest of your life. Job security. It's a long way from writing poetry."

She smiled and he felt like she really got it, really cared. A drop of rain fell on his head. He had a sudden desire to take her in his arms and kiss her. She didn't say anything for a minute. They walked in silence up the hill on Oak Street, past the stone Presbyterian Church, past a little barking white dog. He wondered what he'd say, if someone recognized him. But there was no one in sight. A gust of wind lifted her skirt and she held it down. He felt another drop on his skin.

"It's starting," she said. "My house is just a couple blocks ahead and around the corner." A loud thunderclap ripped the air around them and, in a moment, it began pouring. She reached over and grabbed his hand and they started running, laughing. He almost didn't care if anyone saw him. He hadn't felt so free or so happy in years. They reached her clapboard single story house and rushed up the stairs drenched and laughing and stood panting under the porch roof. She took a key from her pocket and opened the front door, whose paint had started to peel. "Please excuse the mess. Neither of us are very neat."

A light tan colored Siamese cat came meowing up to her and rubbed himself against her legs. "This is Sam," she said. "Sam, Sasha." As if on cue, the cat rubbed against Sasha's wet trousers. "He's my roommate's cat. She's moving soon and is trying to get rid of him. Here, let me take your jacket," she said as he peeled it off. She handed him a large yellow towel and then went to the kitchen to feed Sam. He stood in the hallway drying his hair. He could see a bedroom through an open door, a mattress invitingly on the floor with the sheets pulled back. The house smelled like peaches and vanilla. There was quite a bit of disorder, at least compared to his house.

He noted a guitar in one corner of the living room and an easel in the other. A water color, half finished, rested on the easel of a woman floating on a raft in a river, her head resting on her arm bent behind her, her top half naked, her torso wrapped in a red and blue sari. A photograph of the same scene sat next to it. He walked over towards it as she entered from the kitchen. "Do you paint?" he asked.

"No, that's my roommate's. But it's me, or supposed to be."

He focused on the breasts, perfectly round and pink, and felt his heart rise to his throat. His ears were hot. The woman in the photograph was, indeed, Darlene, though it was less obvious in the watercolor. He turned away from the easel. "Does she play guitar, too?"

Darlene laughed. "No, that's me."

He wasn't sure what to say. He suddenly felt awkward. He tried to imagine what Sarah would say, if she saw him there. It would be Armageddon. It was still so very innocent, though. He could leave now and there'd be nothing at all to feel guilty about. He just got caught in the rain on a walk. They had been talking about Rubashov. He hadn't even smoked the joint he was carrying. That would be proof of his honorable intentions. Obviously, Sarah would see right through all that crap, though.

"Would you like some tea?" Darlene asked.

"Sure. Thanks."

"Herbal ok?"

"Yes, can I help you?"

He walked into the kitchen with her. She set two mugs on a kitchen table covered with a green oilcloth. He sat down on one of the two wooden chairs. She placed a small ceramic bowl with brown sugar cubes between their mugs. A minute later she poured hot water from a kettle and handed him a box of Celestial Seasonings assorted teas.

"Tell me a little bit about yourself. I only know you graduated in Anthropology and work in the library," said Sasha. He was thinking of how really beautiful she was. Her hair was a golden yellow like in a fairy tale hanging in a thick braid down her back. She had bright green eyes and long lashes, and deep dimples on both cheeks that showed when she smiled. He wondered whether he remembered that from their first meeting. She had a gap between her two front teeth. And freckles. It was easy to look at her. There was a softness about her, a roundness, no sharp edges.

"I'm a Leo and a strict vegetarian. I'm hardly out of school yet, so there's not a lot to tell. But I've travelled a lot. I took a year off before graduating and went around the world with one of those one-way tickets, spent a lot of time in India and Thailand. I stayed in an ashram outside Goa for two months and was initiated in a religious order run by a disciple of Sai Baba. That's where I met Rolf, my fiancée," Darlene finished.

Sasha's heart, which had been inching higher in his throat, sunk like a lead weight. 'Fiancée.' The word was like a dagger, deflating the balloon of anticipation, which had threatened to explode. He struggled not to show his disappointment, though part of him also felt a certain relief. "Tell me about the ashram. What did you learn?" he managed.

"We mostly played music and danced or chanted all day. They believe in an ecstatic path to realization. The cause of most suffering, they believe, is the repression of our sensual selves, all the hang-ups and the guilt we learn from the time we are babies. Baba Karma, that's what we called him, not his real name, the leader of the ashram, believes we have to unlearn all the prohibitions and inhibitions we've been taught in order to embrace our true nature. Love is the answer. Whatever gets in the way of love blocks our enlightenment." Her smile was radiant.

Sasha, still reeling, trying to take in all that she said, thought about Sarah. How different his life was from this philosophy! He blamed himself for being so submissive, for not standing up for his true self. Sarah was a total control freak, sexually repressed, but what did that make him? Would he have had the nerve to make love to this girl, if she had been available, as he first thought? he asked himself. He wanted her now, wanted to drop everything and run off to that ashram with her. But he heard himself ask, "Tell me about Rolf."

"Rolfie's German, a Sagittarius, a very accomplished flutist."

Sasha pictured him as Pan, the goat guy, god of the wild.

"I'm going to meet him in Oregon," she continued. "We're helping start a spiritual community with twenty of our friends. We plan to be totally self-sufficient and grow everything we need. It's so exciting. You'd love him"

Sasha couldn't think of anyone he'd like to meet less. Lucky guy. "Starting a spiritual community from scratch sounds exciting," he said. He felt boring uttering these banal clichés. He didn't play the flute or play sports in college and he was married to a woman he had to beg for sex. He was beginning to really hate his life.

"What about you, professor? I know you teach Russian history and you care about big moral questions and you were a beatnik poet in college. What else? Any kids?"

Sasha was surprised by this question. He had even considered taking off his wedding ring when they entered the house, but she had probably already seen that. "No, no children. Just a wife." He couldn't suppress the disappointment he was feeling.

"What's she like?"

He wondered how honest he would be. "Well," he hesitated, "she's a Capricorn, teaches women's studies, is very smart, attractive, has a terrible temper and pretty much lives in her head. She could really use a month or two at your ashram." There it was. It had spilled out. How great to be able to be honest with someone, though. Darlene's face was placid, kind and knowing. She reached over and put her hand on his. He looked up and met her eyes and felt a powerful sensation, an intense feeling of empathy.

"Everyone needs it," she said.

He felt like crying or taking her into his arms. She could see his sadness clearly. Her smile was like a salve. She did not remove her hand. They sat like that for a few moments. It felt perfectly comfortable, as if they were old best friends.

Finally, she spoke. "The first time I met Rolf, I was like that. I judged everything and everybody. I was ruled by my thoughts. I never did anything spontaneously. I didn't trust myself. Rolf taught me to play. He teased me unmercifully until I finally let go. One day we smoked pot together and covered ourselves with body paint and laughed until all my hang-ups fell off of me. The ashram was a safe place to let go. Maybe you'll visit us some day in Oregon and we'll teach you to be a baby again."

Sasha turned his hand over and held hers in it. "Speaking of pot," he said, "I just got the strongest weed I've ever smoked. It's from a former student of mine who moved to California to grow it. It's really unbelievable. Would you like some?" He took the joint out from his pocket.

The sound of the rain on the roof was now a drum beat. She stood up and taking him by the hand, led him to the bedroom. "Remember what we were saying? About lying in bed with a joint when it rains?" she asked. She sat on the

47

unmade bed and gestured for him to do, too. There was a lighter on a bedside table. Sasha took the joint from its bag and handed it to her.

"I warn you. It's strong," he said.

She reached over and kissed him lightly on his lips. His heart seemed to beat louder now than the rain. "What about Rolf?" he whispered.

"That's not a problem," she said. "We have an open relationship. There's no danger for you in any case because I'm leaving here in two months to be with him. We're not officially engaged, but we'll be living together. And you're married, which means there's nothing I have to worry about either. No getting attached, no drama. It's all OK. It's just fun." She lit the joint and inhaled deeply, passed it to Sasha.

He couldn't believe what was happening. All his guilt melted away. The smell of her so close was intoxicating. They didn't take their eyes off each other as they passed the joint back and forth. His head was spinning, his ears were burning, his heart throbbing. She had her hand on his thigh. He held her blond braid in his hand, looked deeply into her eyes, put the joint on the table and leaned towards her. Their eyes stayed open for a moment until their tongues touched, sending an electrifying jolt through his body. He moved closer, their mouths pressing against each other, their tongues probing. His hand moved to her breast. She moved her hand over his crotch, unbuckled his belt and reached for his dick, unleashing it.

Their kisses were frantic now, their faces wet. He got on his knees and took hold of her sweater and lifted it over her head. Her chest was heaving up and down. He reached behind her and unfastened her bra with surprising ease. Her breasts bounced out like fresh fruit. He kissed her nipples gently and then sucked hard on them. She moaned some, then pushed him back a little so she could take off his shoes, socks and pants. Soon they were both naked. Their hands and mouths explored each other. She moved down on him and took him deeply into her mouth while her hand stroked him. He didn't want to come in her mouth.

When he couldn't stand it anymore, he pushed her off of him, turned her on her back and went down on her. The taste of her was like nothing else, some nectar of the gods. He pushed his fingers up her as he kissed and licked and sucked on her clit. It had been forever since he had eaten a woman and he was delirious. Finally, he came up for air and moved to enter her. She reached over to the nightstand and took a condom out from its drawer. She placed it on his erect cock. She held him and guided him inside of her, opening eagerly to him. They looked at each other in wonder and then closed their eyes and rocked back and forth until they both came together with full throated screams. He lay on his back panting, wondering about Sarah and whether his life could ever be the same again. The sound of the rain had stopped.

Chapter 7

They spent the rest of the afternoon and evening in their separate offices on either side of the house preparing for their classes the next day. They were pleasant, but had little to say to each other. That night Sasha was unable to fall asleep. It was if Darlene had awakened him, and now there was no going back. He waited until he was sure Sarah was sleeping and slid from their bed. He went downstairs and made himself a pot of coffee.

Alone in the dark, he felt unglued, not sure what direction to take. The predictability and confidence he had in his life were dissolving. A wave of self-doubt rose in its place. He tried to rationalize his fling with Darlene. He was convinced that it was a kind of necessity, that he was fully justified, that it would ultimately make his marriage happier. But however true these arguments might be, they were not 'get out of jail free' cards that could absolve him of his guilt. Clearly, he wasn't telling Sarah about it because it would hurt her. Would Sarah ever forgive him?

But damn it, he thought. *The reason I can't tell her is because she'd go nuts, the way she always does. It would just make things worse. She'd shit all over me and we'd never get to the reasons why I'd be tempted to have an affair in the first place. That's the real problem. We don't talk about sex. If we could have an honest discussion, we could make changes or come to some understanding. But she'd only see this affair as a betrayal and I'd be branded as an immoral adulterer.*

He could feel his life careening towards a dramatic turning point. It wasn't like he was ever going to leave Sarah for Darlene; she had made it unambiguously clear that she belonged to Rolf and would be out of Sasha's life in a few weeks. Nevertheless, she had revealed to him parts of himself that had long been buried: playful, sensuous and giving; which, now that they were released, made the rest of his life appear bleak, timid and unremarkable. He couldn't see how to reconcile the lover and former beat poet with the sexually repressed tenure track professor. He badly wanted to avoid hurting Sarah. She might not be everything he desired, but she didn't deserve to be humiliated. What could be worse than hurting someone you love? Thank God they didn't have children! But he had to be true to himself. Otherwise, he was a hypocrite and a coward.

At a crossroad in his life, he was utterly stuck. He knew it was bigger than Darlene or even his marriage. Like the country he lived in, he had lost his innocence; but where did that leave him? Who was he? Was there anything about him that was authentic? Why had he always chosen the easy path? Would he grow old complaining about his life, of the roads not taken, like his mother? He wished he had a cigarette, though he had never smoked before. He considered getting drunk, but what good would that do? He picked up a pen that was sitting on the table and on a paper napkin began to scribble incoherent notes in the muted darkness.

How sadly the dew sits on a wilted rose
In the gutters of forgotten dreams
Unspoken fragments of a life unlived
A blind man in a birdcage

He filled several napkins like this with a tiny script in a futile attempt to exorcize the demons he had unleashed. He had a desire to hurt himself, to do anything that might break through his complacency. It had been years since he had attempted poetry, "a hibernation of the soul," he wrote. His anguish was cathartic. He wished he had the courage to go crazy, to do something foolish. He got up and paced around the kitchen. He thought about sneaking from the house and driving to Darlene's. The thought of her curled up in her warm pajamas in bed was almost more than he could resist. But Darlene, he knew, had already purchased her ticket to Portland. She would not be in his future.

He opened a tall cabinet next to the refrigerator and found a half-filled bottle of wine. *What the fuck?* he thought. He pulled the cork and held it to his mouth and managed to guzzle half of it before setting it down. He winced. He had only gotten drunk once, he recalled, when he was fourteen and threw up all over the back seat of Angelo Damien's car on Halloween. He much preferred pot, but the last thing he wanted at that moment was mellow. He wanted crazy. He wanted to break out from himself. He felt the truth of his existence was just beyond his reach, close enough that he could touch it, if he could just pierce the protective cocoon that held him back from his authentic, original self. Darlene had breached his defenses, but it was much larger than her, or Sarah or even sex.

I'm a fraud, he told himself. *Everything about my life is a lie. I'm not the happily married young professor I pretend to be. I'm a frustrated, repressed pseudo intellectual phony. The one honest thing I've done since I got married was to fuck Darlene and I don't have the courage to tell Sarah. I'm afraid of her. Admit it.* He had an urgent desire to confess everything.

He had stopped believing in himself. *I don't actually give a shit about these Russian Communists I profess to criticize. At least they were real men. I've never done anything that wasn't perfectly safe. I've never risked anything in my life. I don't believe in God. I don't believe in anything. I wanted to be a writer, a poet, and ended up writing bullshit academic articles that no one would ever read. I'm pathetic.* He took the bottle and poured some wine into a glass and gulped it. He felt his head start to sway. *What have I ever done that I'm proud of? That guy Carl is real. He's living life. He's fucking living life. I write about freedom as if I actually know something about it, but he's doing it and I'm nothing but a total fraud. I do what society expects of me.*

He thought about his father. He had always been ashamed of him, how he dressed, how he never held a real job. But his father was his own man. He never compromised. He said whatever he felt like, didn't give a shit what anyone else thought about him. *I compromise all the time every day. The way I dress. The people I hang out with. The things I say. Even the way I fuck my wife.* He picked up the bottle of wine and drained it. He stood up and walked outside into the brisk night air. The sky was filled with stars. There was an alley behind the house and he walked through the darkness. He wanted to puke.

He imagined telling Larry that he was quitting his job and heading West to find Carl or to Oregon to join Darlene's spiritual community. Or, he would go to Paris and write poetry. He fantasized killing himself, though he knew he never would. Part of him worried that all this angst was just an act, that he hoped to work himself into such a state that Sarah would have pity on him. How pathetic! How weak he was! How immature!

He resolved to tell Sarah everything. He'd tell Larry first. Larry, at least, would appreciate the balls it took for him to fuck Darlene. Maybe he'd get his own place for a while. Maybe he'd take a leave of absence and join EST or some spiritual community, go to India like Darlene or become a pot grower like Carl. Tomorrow would be another day. Tomorrow he might see Darlene again. He tiptoed back upstairs and slid under the sheets on his side of the bed.

Chapter 8

Sitting at his kitchen table, Larry studied him carefully. "You look like shit, Sash, if you don't mind my saying. What's going on? You and Sarah OK?"

"Mainly, I haven't been sleeping for maybe a month, staying up every night till three or four in the morning writing surreal poetry. He kept his eyes from Larry. "I've discovered I don't like who I am anymore. I feel like a phony. Honestly, I don't know what's with Sarah. We don't seem to talk much anymore. She's got her life and I've got mine."

"I figured something was up with you," said Larry. "I never see you. You're not at the gym and you haven't been available to hike, like forever. What's really going on? I can tell you're hiding something. You got cancer or something?"

A long silence followed. Larry tried to make eye contact, but Sasha kept looking down at the joint that was still burning in an ashtray. Neither of them spoke or moved. Finally, Sasha looked up and met Larry's gaze. Larry could see Sasha's lips quiver. He looked vulnerable, in a way he hadn't seen before.

Sasha stuttered slightly, "I have…wanted to tell you about this. Honestly, though, I've just been too…confused about it. But I can't seem to sort it out by myself." Larry softened his gaze, waited patiently for him to continue. The sound of a large moving van rumbled outside, air brakes squeaking. "I've been seeing someone," he finally admitted. He tried to gauge the effect this had on his friend, but Larry's face remained impassive. "She left this morning. I took her to the airport, cancelled my class."

A slow wry smile began to creep mischievously across Larry's face. "You've been having an affair and you haven't shared any of this with your best friend and therapist? Anyone I know?"

"I doubt it. You might have seen her at the library. She worked at the reserve and research desk. Tall, blond, dimples, green eyes." Larry nodded trying to think if he'd seen her. Sasha continued. "We met there. She was interested in the book I had assigned to my class. She had just graduated and was moving to Oregon, to some spiritual community, to be with her boyfriend. They have an open relationship. I walked her home one day and we ended up smoking some of Carl's pot and making love on her bed. It was the best sex I've ever had. It made me realize how much I was missing with Sarah. I didn't have the courage to tell her, but I'm planning to tonight."

"Oh, shit!" Larry said, closing his eyes.

"We spent the weekend together, the weekend when Sarah and Alice went camping. We just fucked all the time." He paused a moment. "I knew it was just a temporary fling. It had no chance of going anywhere, but I feel like it lifted a veil, made me really look at my life with Sarah, with the university, with the phony intellectual I've become. Everything about me seemed like a lie."

"So, what are you going to tell her?" asked Larry.

"I'll tell her about the affair and what I've begun to learn about myself. If she manages not to go crazy, if we can actually have a real, mature discussion about our relationship, about what we both want from it, maybe there's some chance of saving our marriage. I guess I'll know that when I tell her."

Larry nodded. The moving van across the street released its air. "Look, Sasha," he said, "It's horrible to have to hurt someone you love, but worse to live a lie. Sarah'll get over it. It might be a new beginning, or not."

On the drive home, his mind shifted to Darlene. Surprisingly, he had not thought much about her after he dropped her off at the airport. She had already become a story, something to treasure in his memories; but he doubted they'd ever meet again. He'd miss her. Their lovemaking had turned him on in more ways than one. It had been a month since he and Sarah had made love, he reflected. That had not gone very well. He had been sated after an afternoon tryst with Darlene and it took some effort to get turned on again that night.

He pulled up to his house behind Sarah's car. Then he counted to ten and opened his door. Tiptoeing up the stairs in his house, he could hear Sarah's voice in her study saying good-bye to someone on the phone. Her door was closed. He took a deep breath, then knocked softly.

"Come in," she said. He turned the knob and entered. "I'm not used to you knocking."

"You don't usually have your door closed," he responded. She looked frazzled, distracted. This was not going to go well, he could tell.

"Where have you been?" she asked.

"I was at Larry's house."

"Don't you have classes today?" she asked.

"I cancelled them. It was just too beautiful. I called in well."

He could have lied about that, but even a small lie would compromise the armor of truth he was depending on. To his surprise she didn't react at all, just shuffled some papers around on her desk. He knew she had heard him. It was curious. "How was your day?" he asked.

"It was good. I ran into Ken and Karen. I also took a walk." She paused, "with Alice."

"How's she?" he asked.

"Terrific."

It felt awkward. They didn't have a lot to say to each other lately. There was an air of something stale between them. They had become strangers, he realized. "I've got something to talk to you about," Sasha said at last.

"So do I," Sarah answered, looking up from her desk. "But, please, go ahead."

"No, you first," said Sasha. There was a long fragile silence. Sarah came around from the back of her desk and stood just a couple of feet from Sasha. His heart sunk. He realized that she must have found out. He had wanted to tell her first. Her eye contact was serious, brutal.

"I don't know how to tell you this," she began, "but I'll get right to it." He could feel his heart beating, waiting for the inevitable. "I'm leaving here. I'm going to move into a room at Alice's. Carie is moving out."

He tried to make sense of what was happening. She knew and she was going nuclear right off the bat. He wouldn't try to stop her. It might be the easiest way to handle this.

"Alice and I have become lovers," she said. The words struck like thunder and lightning. He understood what they meant, but it took some time before he realized what she was saying. "Leaving here? Leaving him for Alice?" There was a part of him that wanted to laugh, to laugh at the extreme irony of it all. How many hundreds of times had he imagined the three of them making love? He had encouraged her and now the perversion of his fantasies had struck him in real life. He was turned inside out. The humor in the situation was immediately overwhelmed by a tsunami of hurt. In this game of life, he had lost. It was checkmate. He was stunned, unable to talk.

There were no tears. What could he possibly say? He searched for an appropriate reaction. He had no right to be mad. There was no justice on his side. In fact, he realized he wasn't angry with Sarah at all. He felt like a fool. Just at the moment of his empowerment, he was cut down at the knees. He managed to force a slight smile on his face, more of a smirk perhaps, and said, "I wish you both luck." Then he turned and walked out of her room and out of her life.

Chapter 9

The memory of their last encounter flashed through his mind in a moment, like the scene of a crash one passes on a highway, as Sasha sat down on a log next to Carl. Behind them was the remnants of an old barn with a jerry-rigged 55-gallon steel drum burning scraps of wood to help dry the pot. The barn was crisscrossed with strings spaced six inches apart from which hung two-foot long clusters of buds that were drying. Small scraps of paper separated the different varieties. Carl explained that they were "wet" or "green trimming" the last of their harvest, which lay in large piles in front of them. Most of their remaining crop, he explained, was hanging inside each of their houses. They would be "dry trimming" the last of that in about a week when the pot had sufficiently cured. Everything had been cut down and brought inside and it appeared to be a bigger yield than they had grown previously, he said.

Sasha helped pick large fan leaves off a branch Carl handed him. The top of the branch formed a long cola, like ones he had only seen on the covers of magazines. Once the large leaves were removed, Carl used a small pair of scissors to trim any excess leaf material, shaping a bud that mostly consisted of the resin-secreting flowers that held the psychoactive parts of the plant. Their teacher-student role having reversed, Carl explained that with the prices they were getting, buyers wouldn't want to be paying for the weight of any small sugar leaves that had little THC.

Everyone was mostly quiet while they worked. They separated the trimmings from the manicured buds in cardboard trays on their laps. Trimming was a very meditative activity, especially stoned; and Sasha was seriously stoned. His fingers got so sticky from the resin that it was becoming difficult to separate them. Still, the joints kept coming. When Miriam got up to put her chickens to bed, Carl suggested he and Sasha head back to his yurt and get something to eat. By then the long shadows of late afternoon had begun to give way to a rose-colored sunset. Caliber scampered ahead on the trail to lead them home. The yurt was just a couple hundred yards up the path.

"Holy shit! You really did get some elephant poop," exclaimed Carl, seeing the tarp-covered mound on Sasha's truck. "We'll have to keep that out of the rain till the spring, though it would make a great mulch over the winter. Maybe you could trade Kimmy something for some of it. She's got all the old holes. If you're gonna grow, you'll need to dig new ones. That's the only labor-intensive part of this gig. My grow was hidden up near the spring where we get our water, but I think you could get away with just putting them in the garden by the house. We can talk about all that tomorrow."

The yurt was set on top of a large wood platform that was resting on pier blocks a foot off the ground. A wide deck circled halfway around facing south. There were a dozen steps with tiny risers leading up to it, each just an inch higher than the one below. "To slow you down," explained Carl.

"That's awesome. I could use some slowing down," said Sasha taking one slow step after another.

"You can cheat, if you're in a hurry," said Carl, "take a few steps at a time, but what's the point? Around here there's nothing to be stressed about."

"Except the cops, I guess," said Sasha.

"They pretty much leave us alone. Everyone in these hills is growing now. It's pretty mellow," said Carl.

When they walked into the yurt, Sasha thought he'd entered cannabis paradise. Pot was hanging from every conceivable space. Strings crisscrossed from the walls and the rafters supported foot-long stems of pot drying in rows bunched as close to each other as they could get without touching. The place reeked of marijuana. Sasha wondered whether he'd get more stoned breathing than he would smoking or digesting it. Dry leaves were scattered on the floor, crunching as they walked. "We'll sweep these up tomorrow," said Carl. "They say that you get the wildest dreams you'll ever have sleeping under this stuff." He pointed to a foam mattress rolled up against a wall where Sasha would sleep.

The yurt itself was a 16-foot round structure made of tongue and groove redwood siding. The roof was covered with hand-hewn cedar shakes. Inside, vinyl windows let in light and rafters rose to a large skylight in the middle. There were no interior walls. Carl's bed was on the floor against one wall, a wood burning cook stove and a farmhouse sink on another and a Franklin fireplace that was set back onto the deck so its face was flush with the walls. Caliber had his bed next to it. There was also a wooden table made from an old bowling alley and four chairs. In the middle of the floor there was an antique Oriental rug that Carl had inherited from his grandmother, now well-worn and filthy with pot leaves.

Carl crumpled some old newspapers and started a fire in the fireplace with dry madrone branches for kindling. In a moment, there was a roaring fire that took the chill out of the air. "I need to keep the place warm for the pot to dry; but a wood fire also can take the moisture out too quickly, so I have to be careful not to overdo it," Carl explained. He started a fire in the cook stove as well and put a kettle of water on to boil.

"This here's the hot water tank," he said, patting the side of a galvanized steel tank that stood next to the sink. "Holds sixty gallons. You start your cook stove in the morning, keep it burning, and you'll have hot water all day. There's an outdoor tub and a shower out back." He opened the fire box on the stove, put in more kindling and blew on it to get it going. Pointing inside, he noted, "there're copper pipes coiled inside here that connect to the water heater. Works by convection. It's pretty simple."

"Ingenious," said Sasha.

"Yeah, and free. You can get pretty much everything you need picking things off the ground around here. I'll leave you my chain saw and my split mall, though. You'll need to learn how to chop wood. If you tamp down your fires right at night in the fireplace, you'll have hot embers in the morning and all you'll have to do is throw on some kindling. Kindling's here," Carl said, pointing to a large wicker basket with a pile of dry madrone branches. "All this will probably seem pretty overwhelming at first, but you'll get the hang of it soon enough. You'll have to."

"What's the refrigerator run on?" Sasha asked.

"Propane. The tank's outside. It lasts a month or two, then you take it into town on your truck and get it filled at any of the gas stations."

Carl took a bowl down from a shelf and scooped out some dry dog food for Caliber and added water.

"Who takes care of Caliber when you're gone?" asked Sasha.

"You do," smiled Carl. "Kimmy's got Bruce's dog now."

"Wow! That's awesome!" said Sasha. "I promise to take good care of him." Caliber's ears perked, hearing his name. Sasha patted his thigh and Caliber came over to him for pets.

"He gets a scoop like this each night and two scoops in the morning with a dollop of canned food," said Carl. "He'll protect you, warn you of any danger. When you walk around here be alert to any sounds of rattle snakes. There are plenty of them, but mostly in the summer. Caliber will always find them before they find you, though."

"What about bears?" asked Sasha.

"They won't bother you. I slept in an outdoor bed all summer. They'd come around sometimes, but they don't like the taste of humans." He smiled broadly.

"They're probably a lot nicer than the tenured faculty I'm used to." Sasha laughed.

It was starting to get dark and Carl showed Sasha how to light the kerosene lamps on the table and then hung them around the house. The interior light reflecting off the round walls created a primitive ambience that Sasha recognized, though he couldn't recall where that might have been, a memory that seemed to come from some prior life. "If you want to read," Carl said, picking up a tall, thin lamp with a cotton mesh burner instead of a traditional wick, "this Aladdin is the brightest lamp on earth, but it's also dangerous. It burns super-hot and the wick is extremely fragile. If you look at it wrong, though, it will tear; but it sure puts out light." Carl placed a dish of leftover tofu casserole on the wood stove.

Following him, Sasha asked, "Tell me about the people here and what's going on with you and Kimmy. You seem pretty mellow around each other."

"Yeah. We still like each other. It's no good keeping any grudges up here. Besides, I think this break up'll be good for both of us." They were silent for a minute, then Carl added, "I spent a week with an old girlfriend in Santa Cruz and when I came back Kimmy had moved in with Bruce. They always had the hots for each other. Bruce's girlfriend had left him for a guy named Alan in Alderpoint just the month before."

"Sounds like 'Duck Duck Goose," quipped Sasha.

"Yeah, kind of. From what you wrote me, seems like you had a similar experience with your wife."

"I did. You have to watch what you wish for. I kept fantasizing a threesome with my wife and her best friend, hoping they'd get it on. Well they did, but didn't invite me to join their club."

"Too bad," said Carl.

"But, tell me, how'd this place get started?" asked Sasha.

"Bruce was the first to come up here about six years ago. I guess he knew the nephew of Andy Wallace, who let him stay in an old homestead barn that's since been torn down in return for keeping the road up. Bruce used the wood and an old stone fireplace to build his little cabin. Judge Wallace— he's the Superior Court judge for these parts—owns 14,000 square acres around us and has land that stretches all the way to Wallace Cove on the coast. His family settled this land, which used to belong to the natives. We find arrowheads all the time down by the creek. Then Bruce invited Miriam and the old man here."

"The old man?" asked Sasha.

"Oh, yeah, you haven't met him yet. He's on the last day of a month-long vow of silence, I think. You'll like him. He's 94, an intellectual like you or like you both used to be, I guess," laughed Carl. "His name is Jeffrey Sutherland. Maybe you heard of him. He wrote some popular self-help psychology book in the Sixties, but then dropped out of that world. Used to be the therapist for several celebrities. He won't talk about any of that now, actually won't talk about hardly anything anymore. He thinks that language is some kind of virus that infected people. You'll love meeting him."

"I look forward to it. He sounds fascinating. And what about Miriam? What's her story?"

Carl stood still for a moment, collecting his thoughts. "Miriam, or Meera as we call her, is an enigma; but I probably trust her more than anyone I've ever known. She's got a great heart and the courage of a lion. I don't know what happened to her before she got here. It's all very hush-hush, not something she's ever talked about. But I take it she had a husband or a partner who died. She's not interested in men, or women, for that matter. She likes being independent and self-sufficient. She's the best gardener here. You'll learn a lot from her. I think you two will become good friends."

"That's quite an endorsement," said Sasha. "What an interesting group. Is that everyone?"

"Plus me, but I'm leaving," said Carl. "I don't know when, if ever, I'll come back; but you can have this place for the next year at least. Feel free to grow. Everyone's a grower now. Tomorrow, I'll introduce you to Jeff. You're going to love it here, Professor. I guess I should stop calling you that. People around here don't care what you did before and they don't care what you know. They just want to know that you care. No one living up here takes themselves very seriously."

"That will be a relief," said Sasha.

Chapter 10

Sasha awoke to the soft patter of rain, feeling like he had just had the best sleep of his life. Carl was already up and had started a fire in the cook stove. "Coffee?" he asked.

"I'd love some. How can I help?" He could see his breath. It surprised him how cold it could be at this time of year. *What would winter be like?* he wondered. He moved closer to the stove to warm his hands.

"Why don't you light a fire in the Franklin, if there are any hot coals left," Carl answered.

"Sure." He got dressed in the same clothes he wore the day before. Through the glass doors of the fireplace he could see the fire had gone out. He crumbled up some old newspapers and put a handful of madrone twigs on top and relit it. Mesmerized watching the flames take hold, he kept the damper open until he had a roaring fire going, as Carl had instructed him, then closed it.

He walked outside to the outhouse. The drizzle felt good on his face. The sky was a steel grey, but the ground was covered with oak leaves in shades of brown and yellow. He enjoyed crunching through them, marveling at the silence that amplified the sound of the rain. When he came back inside, Carl threw him a towel to dry his hair and handed him a cup of coffee. Life here had been reduced to its most elemental parts: warmth, shelter, food. There were no distractions, only the silence of small things. In his previous life, he realized, he had never experienced such moments of perfection.

After breakfast, Sasha walked by himself down the path to Miriam's cottage. The rain had stopped and there was a tiny sliver of blue peeking along the ridge where it met the sky. Clumps of tan oaks grew in between patches of bald hills. Beyond that was the Pacific. The path was well worn. Old Douglas Fir trees predominated with intermittent oaks branching out like cursive letters.

Miriam's cabin announced itself with a thin wisp of smoke that rose from a metal stove pipe. As he approached, he saw a brood of chickens scratching in the dirt at some compost that had been tossed on the ground. A sheep, heavy with wool, stood among them looking confused. Close by was an old ping pong table that had badly warped. The top half of a makeshift Dutch door was open. The cabin was essentially an L-shaped addition attached to two sides of a chicken coop. It was made with recycled window sash and doors nailed together with old barn boards of various sizes. The roof was made with metal sheeting covered with several inches of turf. There were wild flowers and iris growing from it. The cottage looked like it had grown up out of the ground.

Miriam's dog, a brown and white mutt, part Corgi, he thought, rushed from the cottage to greet him. When Sasha stopped, she crouched at his feet submissively. He bent down to pet her, then she rolled on her back so he could scratch her tummy. *Quite the intimidating watchdog,* he laughed.

He smelled something baking before he saw Miriam standing over an old cast iron stove. "Come in," she said, not taking her eyes off whatever it was she was stirring. Her voice was deep and melodic. Over red flannel pajamas, she wore an apron with little dogs on it and had on a pair of wool slipper socks. "The dog's Lady Jessica and that's Honey Lamb," she added, seeming to read his mind. "He thinks he's a chicken."

Sasha opened the latch releasing the bottom half of the door and stepped inside. The cabin was warm. Straight ahead of him was a kitchen to his left that consisted of a sink at the far end, a hot water canister mounted with metal bands above it, a half-size refrigerator and a honey of an antique blue wood burning stove with white porcelain enamel doors that were cracked, but serviceable. Pots and pans hung from every conceivable space. On the floor next to the stove was a neat pile of kindling in a basket. On the opposite wall, which was also the back of the chicken coop, were shelves with an assortment of canning jars filled with tomatoes, peaches and peppers. To the right of the door as he entered was a bed on a raised wooden frame covered with a mishmash of colorful pillows. There was only room in the cabin for two people to stand.

"You're just in time for pie," she said, turning to face him. The room smelled of cinnamon and cloves. Their eyes met.

Hers were hazel, more green than brown, her gaze was warm and deep. She had the look of someone who knew herself well: solid, experienced, grounded. Wiping her hands on a dish towel, she stepped towards him and motioned for him to sit on an old upholstered rocking chair that rested by the door. He felt an unfamiliar comfort. She sat on the bed under a single strand of neatly trimmed branches of pot hanging to dry. He looked around at the eclectic art—a watercolor of a woman in a black coat peering out across a misty lake on the wall behind her and an abstract oil painting of constellations of red, purple and green shapes in a whirlwind on the wall across from him. "I feel like I've teleported into a fairy tale," he said. "This is so..." he searched for the right word.

"Quaint?" she offered. "Tiny?" she laughed.

"No, I was thinking more like comfortable, charming, magical."

He felt surprisingly at ease with her in the intimacy of this small space. The cabin, much like Miriam herself, appeared self-contained, sufficient. She could be a witch, he considered, but surely a good witch. She reached for a plate on top of a bookshelf across from Sasha that had a bud and some rolling papers. "Would you like a smoke?" she asked. "It goes well with apple pie."

Sasha smiled. *If only Larry could see this scene*, he thought. "I don't usually smoke before breakfast," he told her, "but I guess I'd better get used to it. Thanks."

"This is sixth generation," she said.

He cocked his head, unsure what she meant.

71

"Each year we select the best female plants and mate them with our best males. We breed for taste, size and potency. One strain might make you laugh or be a strong aphrodisiac, or be more mental. We choose for what we want to preserve. This is my sixth season doing this." As she spoke, she rubbed the flowers of a bud between her fingers and expertly rolled a joint. "Here, taste this." She handed it to him before it was lit. He put it in his mouth and inhaled. "You can taste it better before it burns," she said.

He felt his senses expand as he inhaled the sour, earthy taste of the weed. Miriam had a sly, knowing look, proud of her crop. "Pot reflects the personality of the grower," Carl had told him. The high he felt was strong but mellow, grounding him somehow, but up, happy. "This is nice," he said, smiling at her. Do you ever share your seeds?"

"Only to new friends," she said with a smile. She got up off the bed and moved to the kitchen, took the pie from the oven and placed it on a cutting board to cool. Whatever she was stirring on the stove she poured over the pie. "Coffee?" she asked. "Espresso?"

"Sure."

He watched her as she filled the bottom half of a small, aluminum Italian coffee maker with water and screwed on the top canister with a couple scoops of coffee grounds, inserted a cast iron handle into one of the round grates on the stove top and lifted it, then placed the coffee maker over the exposed hole to percolate. These wood cooking stoves intrigued him. He stood to examine a set of bookshelves by her bed. On the top shelf were hardback copies of Rodale's *Encyclopedia of Organic Gardening* and *Encyclopedia of Composting*, Ruth Stout's *No Work Garden* Book and numerous others like that. But on the bottom shelf, to his surprise, were books by Franz Fannon, Herbert Marcuse and other left-wing intellectual icons.

"Quite an eclectic library you have," he said, pulling out a copy of *The Wretched of the Earth*. "I didn't think people up here would be interested in stuff like this."

She had a wry smile on her face. "They aren't mostly. Those were from a former life. I probably should get rid of them. It's mostly for sentimental reasons that I keep them, I suppose."

"What kind of former life?" he asked.

She seemed suddenly to tighten. The smile dropped from her face. "It's not something I like to talk about," she said, turning back to cut the pie.

He did not persist. They were silent. The hissing sound of the espresso-maker filled the cabin. He put back the copy of *The Wretched of the Earth* and pulled out Frank Herbert's *Dune*. "You like science fiction?" he asked.

"Not usually, but I'm obsessed with *Dune*. It reveals a mysterious, esoteric wisdom that I can relate to, a secret sisterhood that I am drawn to."

"Are there other sisters up here you can share this with? Are you the lone intellectual?"

"Jeffrey and I talk about it all the time. A lot of people have read this, not just the women. I take it you haven't?"

"No, but I had a girlfriend who was infatuated with it, too, so I know a bit about it."

She took the book from him, then handed it back. "Here," she said, "my welcome home present to you."

He was touched. It was not just a book, he realized. She was sharing something sacred to her.

He nodded, bowing to her. "Thank you." He opened it to read. "I'm going to love this. I can tell already. I can't wait to talk with you about it."

She smiled. "You'll enjoy it. There's a lot you can learn from it, if you're open."

"I seem to be nothing but open these days," he laughed.

She turned back to the cutting board and cut two pieces of pie. Not a crumb was out of place. She handed him a piece on a small china plate. "I can see that. Carl told me you were his professor. What made you leave all that behind?"

He took a bite of the pie and his eyes widened. "This is fantastic. And you made this in a wood stove? Impressive."

"Thanks," she said and poured them both a cup of espresso. "You want any cream?"

"No. I'm good." He waited a moment, collecting his thoughts. "I guess I left university life because I felt like a fraud. I realized I wasn't growing anymore. I was acting the part of a professor, a cog in a machine I didn't believe in. The whole university structure is so feudal. Everyone's expected to respect the hierarchy. Academic life is so removed from real life. But it was more than that. I wasn't happy in my own life. My wife and I were going in different directions. There was no passion left between us. She ended up running off with another woman. When Carl offered me the chance to come up here, I jumped at it."

"So, how does it feel to be here?"

He smiled "It's totally liberating. I feel free. I feel like I'm my own self again, kind of like being a kid." He paused for a moment. "And the pie's better here."

Miriam took a lighter, lit the joint again and passed it to him.

"Tell me about Jeffrey," Sasha asked. "Carl said you came up here together?"

"Jeffrey had been my therapist and a close friend. He saved me from a hard time, got me out of a real jam." she said.

"I can't wait to meet him." Sasha said. He wondered what had happened. But she said nothing.

"The past is the past. It doesn't exist," she said. I just don't talk about it. My life's in the present.

"And how's that going?"

"Couldn't be better, actually. I love growing things. And I can get by growing a few pot plants that are worth more than their weight in gold. I grow my own organic veggies and my hens donate their eggs."

"It does feel like Snow White here," he said. "I half expect to see the seven dwarves coming down the path singing, 'Hi Ho, Hi Ho." She smiled. "But what's it like being a woman here all alone?"

"If you mean do I feel safe, I do, completely, at least from human predators. It's not like living in a city. I've done that. I'm never lonely. I love my solitude."

"Are you ever bored?"

She shook her head. The chickens and honey lamb are endlessly entertaining. I read and watch the stars and keep a journal."

They were silent. Pot did that. The movie was inside his head.

After a while, he stood up and put his coffee mug and plate in the sink. Time didn't seem to exist here, he thought. He wasn't keeping her from anything, but he thought he should head back to Carl's to help him with his move, however he could. "Thank you," he said. "I have so much to learn living on the land here. I hope you can help me."

She rose and opened her arms to him. "You are most welcome. I'm glad you're here."

Chapter 11

There was a going away party for Carl the next night at Bruce and Kimmy's hobbit-like house, a round, shingled cabin in a clutch of madrone trees. It had rained off and on during the day and the bare red bark of the madrones glistened like naked legs. Sasha and Carl followed Caliber down a winding path in the early evening as dusk was settling in. A low fog shrouded the tree tops like a baby blanket.

Sasha noticed the crude, but intricately carved wooden osprey that was the handle to the front door. They entered into warmth and the welcoming light of several kerosene lamps hung from exposed rafters. The cabin was pungent with the smell of pot drying on strings. A mobile made from drift wood, hanging from fish lines, rotated slowly above them. The floor was made with wide old-growth redwood planks. The eight-sided, single room cabin was heated by a wood stove fashioned from half an oil drum, which stood in the center of a circle of recycled wood paneled walls and oddly placed sash windows. The random heights of the windows were a bit disorienting at first until one got one's bearings, but they added to the dream-like ambience of the structure. There were more carved animals here and there like the front door handle. An old black cook stove stood against one of the walls next to a deep utility room sink, which he later learned had come out of an abandoned darkroom. On a wall next to the door, were mounted a rifle and shotgun.

At right angles to each other facing the stove were two overstuffed green corduroy couches. Miriam and an elderly bald-headed man in a red plaid wool shirt sunk deeply in one of them. In the other, comfortably curled around himself, was Bruce's grey Australian cattle dog, named Alfie, whose eyes darted alertly from person to person without raising his head. Caliber settled on an oval shaped rag rug by the fire next to Meera's dog, Lady Jessica. Carl walked over to Kimmy and Bruce at the cook stove. Sasha went up to Miriam and the old man.

"You must be Jeffrey," he said, gesturing with his hand out for him to remain seated. The man's head was a bony polished skull with deep furrows, his face was unshaven, but his eyes were as alert as a child's, even as a web of wrinkles radiated from them. He had dark bushy eyebrows, thin pink lips and dimples that widened when he smiled. The man looked up at him and nodded, but said nothing. Miriam scooted next to him to make room for Sasha to sit on the other side of her.

"Jeffrey, this is Sasha, the one we told you about who's going to be living in Carl's yurt," said Miriam. Jeffrey nodded again, smiling.

Sasha smiled back, took his jacket off and sat down. He was conscious of the warmth and feel of Miriam's body against him. Jeffrey kept his inscrutable eyes fixed on him.

"I heard you've been on a speaking fast," said Sasha a bit slowly and loudly, as if Jeffrey were hard of hearing. "I will be eager to hear what you've learned when you're talking again."

Jeffrey smiled more broadly, eyes twinkling and, surprising everyone, spoke with a deep soothing voice like an actor projecting a whisper. "I am now, I suppose. You are graced by my first words in a month." Carl, Kimmy and Bruce turned as one at the sound and even Alfie raised his head.

"I'll drink to that," said Bruce, walking over with a glass of wine in his hand. Gesturing to Sasha, he said, "You've been honored."

"I feel honored," said Sasha.

Kimmy and Carl followed Bruce with glasses and a bottle of Cabernet for everyone.

"A toast," said Carl, raising a glass. "To silence and the wisdom of old men."

"And to you, too," said Bruce, turning to face him. "This going-away party's for you, Carl. We'll miss you."

Bruce lifted Alfie and sat with him on his lap and Kimmy and Carl dropped down next to him.

"I'll miss you, too," said Kimmy, turning to Carl and kissing him chastely on his lips.

Sasha marveled again at how comfortable she and Carl seemed with each other. He wondered whether he and Sarah would ever have that easy a relationship. He flashed on the last thin sliver of hope that she and Alice would welcome him into their bed, but banished it immediately. This obsession would only drag him down, he knew.

"How was it to keep silent so long?" Bruce asked Jeffrey.

Jeffrey cleared his throat. "Well, I must say, it feels very strange to hear my voice again. It's like dying and coming back to life. I learned a lot, learned how silly I am, we all are. Life is just a series of pretensions. Shakespeare was right about us being actors. But, in the end, I admit I was feeling a bit lonely. Coming here tonight was a coming home party for me. It feels good to be here." He paused for a moment, then turned to Carl. "But I will miss you, too, Carl" he said, tipping his glass to him.

Bruce asked Jeffrey, "What did you mostly think about?"

Jeffrey laughed. "I struggled with a persistent voice in my head that insisted on speaking in sentences just as I was struggling to get clear of language entirely. The voice never really learned to shut up, but I found I increasingly could ignore it. It kept butting in to my consciousness, though, always trying to describe my experiences instead of just letting me have them. Alfie understands, don't you Alfie? It's the religion of dogs. But words are good for communicating, I suppose."

"And Scrabble," said Bruce.

"Yes," laughed Jeffrey. "But they get in the way of our direct perception of reality. You'll notice, we don't talk much while we fuck. We should be that way more often."

"Here, here," said Carl.

The conversation soon switched from philosophy to the mundane practicalities of life in the woods, the state of the water line, the culvert that needed repair, the nutritional quality of the dog food they bought. "What are you doing with your come-along?" Bruce asked Carl.

"Selling it, I suppose."

"You ought to buy it from him," Bruce said to Sasha. "It's the best tool you can have up here. It'll pull you out from a ditch."

"No, shit," said Carl. "It saved me many a time last winter. The cars can get stuck up to their axles on our road during rainy season. But you can have it. Call it a long-term loan."

"Thanks," said Sasha, tipping his glass to him. "I'll think of you on the beach in Thailand when I pull myself out of the mud in the rain and cold here."

"Will you be staying all winter?" Miriam asked him.

"I suppose so. I really don't have the money to travel and, besides, I want to experience what it's like here in the winter."

"It's cold and wet, but if you like solitude, it can be wonderful. I'll be here and Jeffrey, too. What about you and Kimmy?" she asked Bruce.

"If my dealer friend gets the kind of price he's asking, we'll go off to Mexico somewhere, probably till March."

"What's he selling it for?" she asked.

"Eight hundred, seven to me. That's twice what we got last year. What about you, Meera?"

"Yeah, it's amazing. I can hardly believe it. Four hundred last year and eight this. Jeffrey turned me onto a filmmaker friend of his in LA who sells to Father Sarducci and the cast at Saturday Night Live."

They all erupted in laughter. "Too bad we don't have TV up here," said Kimmy. "It would be a blast to watch Belushi, knowing he was stoned on Meer's pot."

"I know. I should get a credit. But imagine how our lives would be ruined here, if we had TV."

"No shit," said Carl. They all nodded.

Miriam turned to Sasha. "Jeffrey used to be a shrink in Hollywood. He was Marlon Brando's therapist and other famous actors'. He could tell you stories, but he won't. He was friends with Huey Newton and Eldridge Cleaver, too. I keep urging him to write his memoir, but he just laughs."

Jeffrey shook his head disdainfully. "The game of selves. I'm done with that."

Carl lit a joint the size of a large cigar and passed it to Kimmy. Sasha watched Alfie sniff the air. "Speaking of stars, Daniel finished his portrait of Freewheeling Frank. You should see it before it leaves his studio," said Carl.

"Did Rachel move in with him yet?" asked Meera.

"Yea. And Linda moved in with Ray," answered Carl.

"It's a regular game of musical chairs here," Bruce said to Sasha". "As soon as a couple breaks up, the seats change." Everyone laughed, even Carl.

Duck, duck goose. But not with Miriam, it seems, Sasha thought as he passed the joint to her and wondered.

Chapter 12

Larry,

How are you dude? I've been wanting to write you, but this is honestly the first time I've been straight enough since I arrived. It's been pouring rain the last few days. The relentless pounding on the tin roof of Carl's yurt is quite intimidating, but there're no leaks, not yet. I'm sitting in front of a wood stove that's keeping me warm. It's just getting light outside. It's still warm during the day. By noon I'll be in shorts and a T shirt.

I'm not sure where to begin. Carl left three days ago. I inherited his dog, Caliber, a beautiful yellow lab who is now my best friend. I've only been into this for a few days, but already I'm getting a sense of what it's like to live in the woods by yourself. The yurt is sturdy, well-made. There's definitely a difference living inside a circle. It literally centers you. There's a wonderful wide deck that surrounds the yurt. There's no electricity, though I'm thinking about getting a twelve-volt light, like they sell for RVs, and running a cable from my truck battery. Reading by kerosene lamps is hurting my eyes.

This morning, I caught myself talking out loud. That was quite disconcerting, but I'm learning to know the silence as a friend. It turns everything into a meditation. I am a detached witness to whatever it is I do. The peacefulness is profound. This could get real addictive.

Speaking of that, these people up here know how to grow some wicked pot! There is much I have to learn from them. I couldn't ask for better teachers.

Carl and Kimmy broke up. There was an opening in the dating game and Kimmy went down the path to Bruce's. Apparently, Bruce's girlfriend, Jodi, left him recently for some guy named Alan in town. Someone named Rachel moved in with an artist named Daniel after his girl, Linda, moved in with Ray. I haven't met most of these people yet. Several of them live in Alderpoint, the closest town, which is about 45 minutes from here by car. It's just a post office and a general store. It's also the closest telephone. Up here, we're surrounded by huge cattle ranches and national forest. I can walk 160 miles in one direction and never see another human being. It's hard to exaggerate the beauty of this land. Rolling hills spread out to the horizon. Large open grasslands intersperse with groves of various species of trees.

This morning when I awoke, it was freezing. The fire had gone out during the night. It can get pretty cold overnight. I dragged myself out of bed and tried to restart it. I thought I had that down pretty well, but it wouldn't catch. The kindling was either too wet or too green. Smoke started filling the cabin. I realized I had forgotten to open the damper, but that only helped a little. Crumbling up gobs of newsprint and blowing on the coals until I practically hyperventilated, I finally managed to keep a fire lit. Ten minutes later it caught stride and roared to life, sucking the smoke out, thank God.

The fire in the cook stove was somehow easier to get started, but when I went to get water to boil for coffee nothing came out of the spigot. I had no water. For a moment, I thought my whole move up here was going to collapse around me, that I simply wasn't cut out to live alone in nature so far from urban conveniences. But I quickly convinced myself not to panic. These were all simple things that I would learn to master in time.

The rain had not started yet, so I went down to Bruce and Kimmy's cabin, which is about two hundred yards from my yurt. You remember Kimmy. Bruce is a rough-cut character from Tulsa, a real Okie, but also a cowboy poet and a kind of a folk artist, too. He can fix anything. I can see that I'm going to be totally dependent on him. He doesn't wear shoes, even in the winter. He's about six feet tall and sports a long scraggly beard and has a mirthful laugh. He has no tact, though, so he's apt to say something inappropriate. There isn't an inauthentic bone in his body. He reminds me of a full-sized elf. I like him a lot.

Bruce checked the water in his own faucet. There was only a dribble. His cabin's lower than me, so his runs out last. He dropped whatever it was he was doing when I got there and we headed up the mountain. Along the way, he pointed out the different variety of trees and fauna, warned me to listen for rattlesnakes when the sun came out again and explained how the gravity-flow water system worked, or didn't. A couple hundred yards from my yurt on a small knoll sat a 1000-gallon galvanized water tank. We climbed up an attached ladder and peered inside with a flashlight. It was almost empty. Playful as a child, Bruce made loud noises like a bear that reverberated in the hollowness. We followed the black PVC pipe that snaked up the hills along a small stream. As we climbed, the view expanded below us: overlapping hills cascading to the ocean about 40 miles as the crow flies. Off in the distance there was a herd of deer, maybe thirty of them, more than I had ever seen together before. There were cows, too. What a life they have wandering through thousands of acres of unfenced grasslands. An occasional hawk or crow soared above our heads. But dark, menacing clouds were quickly overtaking the sky.

Every hundred yards or so, Bruce broke the PVC connection, searching for the blockage. On about the tenth try, we found where the flow stopped. Dirt, sand, leaves and air had blocked the pipe there. We unfastened the next lower length of PVC and used pen knife (I now own a pen knife), branches and guile to loosen the debris. A minute or so later, we could hear the sound of water again flowing into the tank below, a very welcome sound. We walked up another 1000 feet to the spring box, which was set in a pool where the spring was widest. We cleaned out the leaves and pebbles that had built up around it.

It's extraordinary to realize where our water comes from and how pristine it is. We take things like water, heat and food for granted in the city. But here, we have a direct relationship to the most elemental parts of life. Yet, it's precisely around these things that my skills and knowledge are most lacking. I feel like an ignorant child next to Bruce. He can rebuild a transmission, operate any piece of machinery or do the work of a plumber, electrician or carpenter. I am totally dependent on him. Lucky for me, he really likes that role. He is always saving people when their cars break down or they're stranded somewhere. I am never made to feel small around him. But I am determined to learn as much from him as I can. I may even start going barefoot, like he does. Walking next to Mr. Natural, I felt silly in my boots, which quickly got soaked in the wet grass. Bruce said it would take me about six months of agony before my feet were tough enough to go anywhere without shoes. But that seemed like a goal worthy of my penance.

We got back to Bruce's cabin just as it started to rain. Kimmy had made a pot of hot chocolate and we sat around their makeshift wood stove, which Bruce had welded from an oil drum and a strange assortment of parts, and talked about the characters I would meet. I've already met everyone up here. Miriam lives by herself in a tiny room she built onto the back side of a chicken coop not far from Bruce's cabin. She's a dark, intriguing woman, possibly the most composed, self-sufficient person I've ever met. Apparently, she's the best gardener in these parts, so I'm hoping she'll teach me all that I need to know. She grows some amazing weed. I get the impression that she once may have been a New Left intellectual, but she's a born-again, back to the land hippie now and refuses to talk about her past.

Kimmy, as you'll undoubtedly remember, is blond and cute and pretty shy, though opinionated. I can't quite figure her out. I think I might intimidate her somewhat since I used to be her history teacher in my former life. She keeps her distance. When we speak about Meera, she often has something sarcastic to say. I get the feeling that Kimmy feels like Meera looks down on her or it might be that she sees Meera as a future competitor for Bruce. Or maybe it's just that Meera seems so mature, so confident of herself, that Kimmy feels like a kid around her. Whatever it is, she makes fun of Meera's reluctance to talk about her past and the drama built up about the apparent death of her husband, all still very mysterious.

But Kimmy doesn't have a bad word for Jeffrey Sutherland, the "old man," as they call him. Apparently, no one does. He's 94 and pretty much stays to himself. He's not so much a patriarch for this merry band of dope growers as he is their avuncular mascot. They keep him on a pretty high pedestal, though. I get that he came up here to help Meera escape from someone or something and decided on the spot to give up his very public life. His books, it seems, were pretty popular with a certain sub-set of Bay Area hippies, LA actors, black nationalists and acid heads. I think I may even have seen a copy of one of them on your shelf. He had intended to come up here for a week or so, but never returned to the city, not even for a day. It's interesting to learn the path that each person took to get here.

Bruce's story is interesting. He was married, working as a mechanic in Tulsa. One day he comes home early and finds his wife in bed with his best friend. He didn't get mad. He simply handed the guy his keys and told him, "Here're the keys to my house and my truck. You can keep them and my wife. All I want is your Harley." He traded him, got on the motorcycle and drove to California.

And here I am, the ex-assistant professor of Russian history, totally unprepared for living alone on the land. The only use for my dissertation on *Bukharin's Theory of Equilibrium* would be in the outhouse. But I'm loving the life here. I feel so free, so authentic. There are none of the normal distractions I'm used to. Everything is reduced to the essentials of living. There are no pretensions. The rhythm of life is slow and easy. Time is a function of the sun and moon, of light and dark. Nature is not something abstract, not a commodity, not something to even preserve. It's what's all around me and what I'm now a part of. When I heard an owl hooting last night as it was getting dark, I felt like kin. Brother owl was discoursing about something. Maybe someday I'll learn to understand what it is.

It feels good to write to you. I hope someday you'll come visit. I miss you, but not anything else about the life I left. Please write me back. It will mean a lot to me.

Your buddy, Sash

Chapter 13

It rained for a week straight. The wood that Carl had left him was running low. He would have to go out soon with the chain saw and cut some more, wet or dry. Inside the yurt, though, it stayed warm and cozy. With the pot out of the house, the smell of moist earth and smoke filled the space. He curled up with Caliber on the rug in front of the fireplace waiting for the cook stove to get hot enough to boil water for coffee. His days had become routine. It took some getting used to living without clocks. There was nothing to get done except cook, eat and stay dry and warm. He had never spent so much time alone.

At last he heard the rattle of the tea pot and got up off the floor to make coffee and feed Caliber, who waited excitedly by his feet. He put on some oat meal to cook, adding raisins and cinnamon. He thought about his day. If the rain let up, he might cut down a tan oak he spotted close to the road that had fallen. He was anxious to try out Carl's chainsaw. Everything he did was a test. Everything was new. He tried several times to write, but it all seemed pretentious. He did not have the skill to convey the truth of what he was experiencing: the feeling of awe listening to the relentless rain on the metal roof, the joy of completing simple tasks, the strange satisfaction of overcoming his loneliness.

He thought a lot about Darlene, surprisingly little about Sarah. The pot made him horny. He played with himself a lot, but the law of diminishing returns had its effects. It worked, though, to get his heart beating in the morning and motivated him to get out of bed. The slowness of brewing coffee was a meditation. With a fire going all day, he got into baking bread, beating the batter by hand, letting the yeast rise in a covered bowl near the stove. The smell was intoxicating.

He let Caliber outside and started a set of tai chi in front of the fireplace, a practice he had learned from a young Chinese student when he was in graduate school. That all seemed so long ago now. His movements were slow and deliberate. It was the only time, he reflected, when he felt graceful. He no longer had to think of his next move: he simply watched as muscle memory "moved hands like clouds." Sometimes his mind would wander and he'd forget where he was in the set. If he kept going, his body would usually continue without him and his mind would soon catch up. But if he hesitated, if he thought too much, he'd be lost and forced to start again from the beginning. When he did it perfectly, he felt confident his day would go right.

Today was perfection, his best yet. He was moving in slow motion. He had started adding sitting meditation to his morning practice. He sat on the one comfortable upholstered chair and closed his eyes. He had never been able to sit cross-legged. His feet were pronated from birth and his pelvis was hopelessly turned in. But on this chair, he could settle in and let his mind and body relax. At first, he listened to the rain, but soon his mind wandered to the wood he would cut, to plans for building a chicken coop, to Miriam, and each time he told himself to let these thoughts just pass by like smoke, and focus, instead, on his breathing. Without a clock, he had little idea how long he had sat there, but probably twenty minutes, he thought.

He got up and went to the sink to shave. There was a small framed mirror tacked above the bowl, the only one in the yurt. He had been considering whether to let his beard grow like most of the men around there, but not now. The water was warm, but hadn't gotten really hot enough yet, so he put a stopper in the sink and added boiling water from the kettle. For the past week, he had gone without shoes, though he was mostly forced to stay inside. When he did go out, as he would now to the outhouse, he reveled like a child, feeling the mud squoosh between his toes. He had already cut and bruised his feet enough, though, to know what an ordeal it would be to toughen them up to walk on anything; but he had determined that this would be his rite of passage to a new life.

He ate his oatmeal with some maple syrup and homemade yogurt that Meera had given him. Meera intrigued him. There were things she wouldn't discuss, emotional scabs she'd rather not pick at. He couldn't figure out his feelings towards her. He found her very attractive in an elegant, graceful way, that hinted at good breeding. He was surprised when he learned that her parents were Lebanese immigrants who came to this country when Meera was barely a teenager. She went to public schools in Baltimore, then Goucher College and spent a year at the University of Maryland Law School. But history seemed to stop there.

Meera was smart, a good listener, a serious person. It took a lot of courage, he thought, for a woman to live alone in the woods, but she had developed an impressive set of skills. She had built her little cabin by herself. Her garden was the envy of everyone and, most importantly, she seemed to have fully come to terms with herself. There was no yearning for something different, be it lovers or travel or adventure of any kind. She was fully self-sufficient, complete. Her world worked.

Sasha was attracted to her, but it found no reflection and he had to accept that this important relationship could only survive as a platonic friendship. And so it was. He envied her. He felt unfinished by comparison. He still wasn't sure what he wanted out of life. He struggled to accept what he had as enough. He remained spiritually restless, even as he settled into the peacefulness of his new life.

The hard rain slowed to a steady patter and Sasha took advantage to run to the outhouse. A three-sided wood shed with a shingled roof, it enclosed an elevated wooden platform over a large hole in the ground with an oak toilet seat to sit on. There was a bucket with wood ash from the fireplace to pour in the hole after use. It was surprisingly effective at keeping the odor to a minimum. On one wall Sasha had hung his framed

university diplomas. The view from the open front was
sublime. Sasha felt like he was sitting on a throne. He was
most at peace here, protected from the rain and surrounded by
nature's beauty.

By the late afternoon, the rain finally stopped. Leaves
dripped. The angry sky lifted its skirt near the horizon. He
poured a can of oil into a two-gallon gas can and put it in the
back of Tuffy, along with the Stihl, and shut the tailgate with
a determined clang. Carl had shown him how to prime the
chainsaw, choke it and get it started, but Sasha had not used it
yet. That morning he filed each tooth of the chain with a
device that sharpened them to even angles. It had taken quite a
while, but he wanted to make friends with it. He adjusted the
tightness of the chain so it lifted off the guide bar just a half
inch or so, as Carl had taught him. He felt ready, but he was
nervous, knowing how dangerous the tool could be.

He left Caliber inside the yurt and drove down the drive,
flooded with testosterone. This was real man stuff, not like
marking papers. Tuffy clanked and roared like a machine gun,
swerving from side to side on the muddy road. It powered
through pot holes the size of small cars, sending sprays of
water to either side. This was like going into battle. He spotted
the tan oak lying on its side up the hill above the road, which
would allow him to roll the rounds down to his truck. When
he turned the engine off, the sound of silence filled the air.
Sasha felt more alone in this vast empty space than he had ever
felt before. He felt the forest watching him. He lifted the Stilh
and the gas can from the truck bed and pretended confidence

as he strode up the hill. Today he would wear his boots. Even Bruce would do that.

The fallen tree trunk was about three-feet wide at its base, which was half buried in the wet earth. But its upper half was safely off the ground, suspended on some of its larger branches. Sasha put the chainsaw on a dry patch, placed his left foot through the handle opening, pressed the plastic primer pump, choked it, and with a prayer, pulled on the rope. Nothing. He pulled and pulled till he exhausted himself. He sat on the ground panting. He didn't care how wet his jeans got. He reviewed everything Carl had told him, then got up to try again. Suddenly it hit him what the problem was. He had forgotten to turn the little power switch on. He laughed at himself. A crow cawed, mocking him.

Round two. Switch on, everything ready, sounds of a motor struggling to turn, but still no success. He could tell it was flooded. He decided to wait. Looking around, he felt at one with the world. Despite his mechanical armaments, his existence was insignificant in this vastness. Yet, he felt comforted in the presence of something so much greater than himself. No matter how small and irrelevant he might be, he was a part of it, in life and in death. There was nothing separating him from the tree that had fallen and the gift of warmth it would give him. It was one story.

When enough time had passed, he diligently followed the routine and pulled on the rope again. Once, twice, three times and, miraculously, on his fourth pull, the engine turned over and roared to life. He turned down the choke and the saw purred obediently, vibrating in his hands. His excitement rose. He started at the top and sliced off branches with stunning ease, working his way down the girth of the giant. He left the large branches that kept the trunk off the ground and returned to the top and sawed off small rounds that fell submissively by his feet. The sound was offensive, but satisfying at the same time. The efficiency of those swirling steel teeth impressed him. His blade got stuck on a knot in the trunk, but, with much struggle, he managed to work it free and moved just south of it. He was feeling buff.

On the next cut his blade got crimped and did not go all the way through. He pulled it back out and attacked from underneath with the top of the bar's nose. It started to saw through the last few inches easily and then suddenly kicked back. Sasha threw himself backwards to the ground, dropping the saw next to him. It stayed on, moving ominously like a hurt animal on the wet ground. Chastened, Sasha picked it up and started cutting again, more carefully now. He tried to lift the remaining trunk to place a round underneath. He didn't want to saw into the dirt. But it was too heavy to budge. He kept sawing. When the machine ran out of gas, he filled it again. His ears were ringing. He was feeling victorious. As he walked back to the trunk, holding the saw running in one hand, he slipped on a wet branch and fell. The blade, still turning, cut his jeans at the crotch. He turned it off and pulled down his pants. He wasn't even scratched, but it freaked him out.

That would be it for the day, he decided. He rolled the cut rounds down to the road, some of them crashing against

Tuffy. The wood was heavy from the rain. Soon, the truck bed was filled. Tuffy started with ease and rode down the road with pride. The stick shift rattled, the engine struggled with the load, but Tuffy powered on eagerly. Rather than travel the three miles to the county road, Sasha decided to try to turn around at the nearest wide spot. He maneuvered forward and back, but his rear passenger side tire soon started spinning. He rocked the truck, but it only made matters worse. Then he remembered Carl's Come Along that was buried under a cord of firewood.

He began pulling the rain-soaked rounds from one side of the bed until he could see the steel Come Along and pulled it out. He had never used this tool before, but it appeared to be pretty straight forward. There was a cable with a large hook on the end that was on a spool that could be released by a small ratchet on a lever. He let out some of the cable and wrapped it around the axle nearest to the stuck tire and hooked the other end of the device to a nearby tree. He only needed to move the truck a couple feet to extricate it from the hole it had made. Each pull on the long handle drew the cable tighter, but after he took up the slack, nothing budged. He tried and tried and finally gave up.

Defeated, he walked back up the road. It had started to rain again. His boots were clogged. His clothes were wet. He was getting cold. Every once in a while, he'd look down at the slit near the zipper of his jeans and wondered, if he were cut out for this life. He was so completely out of his element. He felt lost. His optimism deflated like a balloon. When he finally got back, he went straight to Bruce's, but no one was home.

He walked over to Meera's and found him there having a cup of espresso. They laughed at him, especially when he showed them the cut in his pants. "Come on, professor," let's pull you out. The name stung, but Sasha laughed with them. All three of them piled into Bruce's truck, an old Ford half-ton, and soon came to the scene of the crime.

"You tried the Come Along with all that wood in the back?" Bruce asked. He had a way of making fun of people with a playful lightness that didn't hurt. There was no malice. He just found everything amusing. Because he never took himself seriously, no one felt judged. They all helped unload the truck. Meera laid chains from the back of Bruce's truck on the ground in front of the stuck tire and then, while Bruce operated the Come Along, Meera and Sasha pushed from the rear. It only took a minute to muscle the truck back onto the road. They all helped load Sasha's truck again. He felt pretty foolish until Bruce said, "This is a great pile of wood you got there. Nice work, Sash."

Chapter 14

Thwap! The 16-pound maul split the oak round in two. There was nothing more satisfying, Sasha thought, than cleanly splitting wood on the first swing. He bent down and picked up one of the halves and balanced it standing up on the stump that was his chopping block. Lifting the maul again, he aimed for a small crack that ran across the grain. He raised the split maul high above his head and, sliding his right hand down as he shifted his weight, brought the full force of the maul down on the log. This time he missed the crack. The maul stuck in the wood. It took some effort to pry it loose. It was all a meditation, he told himself. *Keep your eye and your mind on the spot you are aiming at, nothing else. Be one with it.*

His mind went back to a time in high school when he wanted to join a golf club, but his parents couldn't afford it. He had gone with some friends to a driving range and became enthralled with the challenge of hitting that little white ball. He was convinced that the proper attitude would yield perfection. It was a matter of attention and discipline. If he could hit it well once, he should be able to do it most of the time. Chopping wood was the same. He just needed to apply the principles of tai chi that he practiced each day. "Not to use unnecessary strength," his Chinese friend repeated endlessly to him. Strength was not the key. Let the maul do the work. The skills of tai chi, shifting weight from one foot to the other and pivoting from the hip, should apply to chopping wood. It all came down to practice.

He noticed that he was getting stronger. He had gained a few pounds. The last two months had begun to change him. His upper body, particularly, showed more lean body mass, more definition. His shoulders were wider. Though he still shaved, he had let his hair grow long, which he now tied in back with a leather strap. He had changed in other ways as well. With each new skill he learned, his confidence grew. His gait was more determined and his posture straighter. "Heart to the sky," he could hear his father's voice telling him. But the biggest change, he thought, was getting out of his head, of seeing what was around him.

He had learned to appreciate the long days and nights when there was no one around. Bruce and Kimmy had left for Mexico and Costa Rica and there remained only Jeffrey, whom he rarely saw, and Meera, whom he visited with most days. When Meera left to visit her parents in Baltimore for a week, he was virtually alone. There was little to do but try to understand his place in the universe. He found himself in an almost constant dialogue with God, or whatever it was that determined the laws of nature. He became fascinated by the inherent intelligence of plants, their various survival strategies.

He even wrote a polemic titled, "We Must Conspire Like Plants for Our Survival," but threw it away. He was increasingly drawn toward Native American philosophies of living with nature.

Tonight, he had invited Meera and Jeffrey over for a post-New Year's Eve dinner. It seemed none of them had realized what day it was until a couple days had passed. He had baked bread and prepared everything for a chicken stir fry, which he'd cook in the wok. He almost called off the dinner when Caliber got skunked the day before, but the smell had mostly dissipated by now. Meera helped him rub V8 Juice on the dog, there being no tomato juice to be found. But it worked.

The sun was just dropping behind Grizzly Mountain casting long shadows when he saw Jeffrey and Meera walking arm in arm up the path. She was carrying her signature pineapple upside down cake covered with a checkered cloth. She had dressed for the occasion, looking very attractive in a long skirt and form fitting sweater. Jeffrey was holding a bottle of cabernet. They mounted the twelve short steps like Zen priests up to the deck and embraced him. "Happy New Year," said Meera. They all laughed.

"You know, I hated New Year's before," said Sasha. "There were too many times when I didn't have a date or I had one and she showed more interest in someone else. It brings back bad memories of loneliness."

"And now, you live in loneliness," reflected Jeffrey.

Sasha laughed. "I do and I mostly love it." But he thought of a letter he had written a week before to Darlene. He hoped he had the right address for her commune in Oregon. He had told her about his new life and urged her to visit.

Meera handed him a small, flat package wrapped in newspaper. "I have a present for you." He unwrapped it. In a small silver frame, she had written:

Fear is the mind-killer.
Fear is the little-death that brings total obliteration.
I will face my fear.
I will permit it to pass over me and through me.
And when it has gone past I will turn the inner eye to see its path.
Where the fear has gone there will be nothing.
Only I will remain.

"Oh! Thank you so much. This is the essence of the book, the real secret of the Sisterhood, isn't it?" exclaimed Sasha.

"It is, indeed," added Jeffrey. "You can learn a lot reading *Dune*. Lots of people think it's all a parable about LSD. Perhaps the spice is meant to convey that, but it's much deeper."

"How's Caliber?" Meera asked. Sasha had left him outside with Lady Jessica on the deck.

"Oh, the smell's mostly gone now. He's stopped rubbing himself on every surface. That V8 did the trick." But it reminded him to light a stick of incense that he poked into an orange. "This should cover anything that might remain."

They sat at the table. Meera rolled a joint. Sasha brought over some glasses and a corkscrew and a plate of pecans and lit a couple kerosene lamps.

"These are great," said Meera. "How'd you make them?"

"I just soak them overnight and then leave them in a warm oven till they're ready, like this."

They passed the joint and Jeffrey poured them each a glass of wine.

"How come you don't have a dog, Jeffrey?" Sasha asked.

"After Mary died, I didn't want to get attached to anyone. I used up my store of grief, I suppose. There was nothing left in the account. I had no choice but to learn how to live alone. You see, I've outlived all the family and friends I ever loved," Jeffrey said.

"Except me," Meera corrected.

"Yes, dear, except you. But you will certainly outlive me. This could be my last New Year's. Good riddance, I say. I'm like you Sasha, never liked it."

Sasha and Meera didn't say anything. There was an awkward moment of silence. Sasha stared at Jeffrey and wondered. His body had diminished even in the short time since Sasha had arrived. His mind was sharp, but he seemed tired.

"Tell me how you met Mary," Sasha asked. "What was she like?"

Jeffrey's smile filled the space between them. Memories of her was the elixir of his life now, whatever was left of it.

Sasha turned to Meera. "Did you know her?"

"No, she died just before Jeff and I came up here."

After a moment, Jeffrey continued. "It was Beverly Axelrod who introduced us. We were good friends. I had been working with her, trying to help her quit a terrible cigarette

103

habit. It eventually killed her. Emphysema. Beverly was a brilliant lawyer, the head of the Lawyers' Guild in San Francisco. She fell in love with Eldridge Cleaver when he was in jail and managed to get him released. *Soul on Ice* is a collection of their love letters. Eldridge and Huey Newton started the Black Panthers in Beverly's apartment. That famous photo of Huey in a rattan throne chair? That was Beverly's, in her living room. It soon became an embarrassment, though, for the Panthers that their leader was living with a white woman, a Jewish white woman, no less. They arranged for him to marry Kathleen. Eldridge was a great writer, you know. He told Beverly he had to decide whether to become the next James Baldwin or the next Malcolm X. If Baldwin, he could stay with Beverly and not give a fuck what anyone thought. But he chose Malcolm, ego over id, I suppose."

"Where did Mary fit in?" asked Sasha.

"Mary Escher was one of Beverly's best friends. After all the shit that came down around the Panthers, Beverly left by boat with her dog Pooh for London. Mary house sat for her. When Beverly got to London the authorities wanted to quarantine the dog for two months, so Beverly searched for some place she could go and ended up living with Pooh in Grenada for two years. Before she left, she introduced me to Mary."

He paused for a moment. "You asked 'What was she like?' Well, she was very beautiful—twenty years younger than me—and extremely shy. It was hard for her to be around more than one person at a time. She was a very talented artist. Her oil paintings, mostly portraits of famous Bay Area musicians, had attracted quite a following. But success frightened her and she feared it would prevent her from doing new things. Then, just as she moved away from representational art and into abstract painting, she began to show symptoms of early onset Alzheimer's. I took care of her as long as I could, but every day she regressed more and more. I couldn't leave her alone for a minute. She was like a three-year old when I finally had to put her in a home. I had given up my practice and pretty much everything else in my life. But then Meera's husband, whom I was very close to, died and we came up here together to grieve."

Sasha looked at Meera. Her expression was inscrutable. She did not break eye contact. He would love to know what she was thinking and feeling. The mystery of her attracted him, her combination of gravitas and grace; but he had not yet found any vulnerability, could not find that crack that ran across the grain of her beauty.

Chapter 15

A brittle, reverential silence followed. Sasha understood there would be no further talk of Jeffrey's wife or Meera's husband, at least not tonight. Jeffrey reached for the joint and lighter that lay on a clay plate, lit it and passed it to Sasha.

"We were as green as you are now," Jeffrey said. "If it weren't for Bruce, I don't know how we'd have survived. He taught us everything."

Sasha inhaled deeply and passed the joint to Meera. "Seems like you led a big life before you came up here, Jeffrey. Was it hard to give it up?"

"Not at all. Didn't miss it for a second. When you're in the middle of it, all that flash and noise seems so important. Being here, you realize how vain it all was," Jeffrey said with a hearty laugh. "I was a great name dropper in my time, knew all the pretty people, but I doubt any of them could have pulled me out of the mud like Bruce did for you the other day."

Meera passed the joint back to Sasha. "Jeffrey was a pretty big deal, a star in the San Francisco social scene. Even Herb Caen wrote about him," she said.

Jeffrey shook his head and laughed. "I spent the first part of my life becoming a somebody and the last part becoming a nobody. Somebodies are always chasing after illusions. They're never satisfied. There's never enough fame or money or power. Becoming a nobody, though, can be a spiritual journey of self-discovery. It's an opportunity to discover who you really are."

Sasha smiled. "I guess I never really bought into the whole university status game. I always felt closer to the students than I did to the tenured faculty. It was a relief to leave there. I hated the pretentiousness."

"It's hard to be pretentious here," laughed Meera. "We're all pretty equal."

There was a sudden loud knock at the door and a young man with a crazed look in his eyes entered carrying a rifle in one hand and a dead porcupine in the other. He had hair to his shoulders and a large drooping mustache. He looked like old photographs Sasha had seen of Wild Bill Hickcock. He was smiling from ear to ear, revealing a mouth full of missing teeth.

"Charles, where've you been?" exclaimed Jeffrey.

"Here and there. I caught me a porcupine. Ever had porcupine stew, Jeff?"

"Can't say I have."

"I'll skin it and we can cook it tomorrow with some vegetables and potatoes. It ain't no sirloin steak, but it's some good protein and doesn't taste too bad," the young man said. He was dressed in a camo jacket and pants and never stopped smiling. He put his rifle down, leaning it against the wall, and walked over to Meera who handed him a joint, then turned to Sasha. "You the professor friend of Carl's?"

Before he could answer, Meera said "Charles meet Sasha. Sasha, Charles." They shook hands. "Charles was born and raised in these woods, knows more about the animals around here than anyone. He can find his way through the forest at night and tell you every animal that passed by there in the last couple days. You should go hunting for arrow heads at the creek with him sometime."

"I would really love that," said Sasha. "I heard about you. Carl said you knew all the secrets up here, where all the bodies are buried."

"I can show you where the Indians camped and where they were massacred, if you want. There are still some human bones buried there. You wouldn't believe it."

"Charles is an amateur anthropologist, you might say," said Jeffrey.

"What's for dinner?" asked the young man.

"Chicken stir fry and cake. Would you like some?" offered Sasha.

This rough young mountain man was probably in his twenties, thought Sasha, though it was hard to tell. He had a couple scars on his face and a deep wrinkle that seemed to divide his brow in two and a gold tooth. His eyes were pale blue and narrow. There was something lovingly tender about him, though, a boyishness beneath the surface that seemed to need mothering. Sasha was immediately drawn to him.

Jeffrey took the joint from him, inhaled and passed it back. "Charles, we were just having a discussion about somebodies and nobodies. Tell me, what do you think's the measure of a man? How do you judge someone?"

Charles looked around, making eye contact with each of them. "I don't judge nobody. If people are kind to me, I'm kind back. You can tell a person by the way they look you in the eye. I know animals and how they'll act; but people, you can't be too sure of. Hippies are different than most, though. You all seem to be pretty harmless," he shrugged. He served himself some of the stir fry and, lifting the plate to his mouth, shoveled it in with a few big spoonfuls.

"Time for cake," said Meera. She got up and came back with her upside-down cake.

Charles turned to Sasha. "So, you gonna grow some weed?"

"I hope so," said Sasha.

"What you using for seeds? I got some killer purple cross, 8th generation, I'd be happy to give you."

"I'd love that," said Sasha. "Thank you."

As they ate their cake, Sasha and Meera made eye contact. The inscrutable look she had given him before had become a warm smile. She seemed to be sizing him up. He smiled back and their smiles brightened, as if they shared an unspoken intimacy. Sasha didn't know what to make of it, but it made him feel shy. He did not look away.

Meanwhile, Charles continued recounting stories of people who had lived and died on the mountain, brought them up to date with news and gossip from town and regaled them with unknown facts about the behavior of bears. Suddenly, there was an explosion in the Franklin fireplace, followed by a roar. They all jumped up at once. Charles laughed. "Chimney fire!" he exclaimed.

Sasha was terrified, afraid Carl's house would burn down, but the others didn't seem as concerned. They ran out to the deck and watched sparks flying from the chimney. "What can I do?" asked Sasha. It looked like the eruptions on Mount Etna he had seen in Sicily.

"Nothing, really," said Meera. "It's a good way to clean the creosote from the chimney. Just get ready in case any of the embers catch fire. The roof's metal, so there's not much of a problem there. Probably a good idea to clean the chimney from time to time, though."

"Yeah," said Charles. "Just go up there with a long chain sometime and twirl it around and you'll knock the creosote off the sides. Makes quite a mess, though."

The sparks erupting from the chimney made for a beautiful fireworks display floating up towards a sky filled with stars. Sasha felt a profound gratefulness. Life up in the hills had a certain tenuousness to it, but the hyper reality of living in nature made him feel more alive than ever before. He looked over to Meera who was staring at the heavens and allowed himself to take in her beauty. She had a lovely figure, he reflected, and the posture of someone who was comfortable in her skin. But it was a dispassionate judgment, he told himself. He would not let her physical attractiveness compromise their friendship. His mind turned to Darlene.

Chapter 16

Sasha awoke in the dark to the sound of Caliber whining and scratching at the door. *Something's out there,* he thought. *I hope it's not another skunk.* The moment he opened the door, Caliber bolted, barking ferociously, headed towards the outhouse. Sasha watched him plunge into the woods. He could see something big crashing through the brush in a hurry. Naked, Sasha followed at a distance with a flashlight to get a closer look. It was a black bear, he saw, probably an adolescent, he reckoned. Climbing a fir tree with alacrity, the bear looked forlornly over his shoulder at Calber, barking triumphantly below him. Sasha shined his beam on the embarrassed bear who climbed higher still. Two yellow discs reflected the light, an eerie sight in the dark night that sent a shiver down Sasha's spine. He was excited, but listened carefully for sounds of any other family members that might be nearby. Too cold at last, he retreated to the yurt, leaving Caliber and the bear to figure it out themselves. Stopping by the sink for a drink of water, he heard an empty rush of air. He would have to head up the mountain in the morning to fix the line.

He woke up again at daylight, feeling refreshed. Caliber was asleep by the door. He let him in and fed him dry food. "Sorry, dude. There's no water. This'll have to do for now. I'll get you a bone when we go into town to celebrate your treeing that ole bear. Good job." He petted him and made a mental note to leave a gallon of water for times like this.

Starting a fire in the cook stove, he realized he was wasting his time, there being no water for coffee. He got dressed, put on a jacket and headed up the trail that wound its way around the little pond and up to the bluff with the water tank. There was no sound of water splashing into it. He didn't bother to climb the ladder. He knew the tank would be empty. With Caliber running ahead, he followed the black pipe a hundred yards up the mountain and pulled two sections apart from each other. Nada. He climbed higher and higher until he finally found one with water flowing abundantly through it. He unloosened the mud and debris that had clogged the next lower section and sat in silent anticipation of hearing the clanging splash of water finally empting into the hollow galvanized tank below. He felt proud that he knew how to do this and looked down at his poor battered feet and smiled. Finally, there came the satisfying sound of water flowing with gravity's grace, as if a gift from God. When he looked down at the tank, he saw Meera waving to him.

She signaled for him to wait there. He sat on an outcropping of rocks adorned with a lone buckeye tree, an island on a sloping hill of grasses, and looked out over the receding hills, their valleys wrapped in pink ribbons of fog, the bottoms of lazy clouds illuminated by the morning sun. It would be a beautiful day. Sunlight crept up the mountain like a woman lifting her skirts to welcome the day. Caliber ran down to greet his friend Lady Jessica. By the time Meera reached Sasha, he was sitting in full sun.

"Look what I found," she said, holding something in her hand. She opened it to reveal a small white flower. "It's a crocus," she exclaimed, "the first sign of spring. I found it by the tank." Meera was dressed in a blue print dress with a puffy down jacket and hiking boots. For the first time in days, she did not see her breath. There were signs of new grass all around them. The earth smelled sweet. "It won't be long now," she continued.

"I'm ready," he answered. "I've had my share of cold."

"Hey, thanks for fixing the water line. For some reason I dread doing it," she said. "I was planning to make you a coffee cake, this morning."

"How very kind," he said. "Why don't you come to my house? The morning's just beginning. It won't take too long to get some water. I'll make an omelet, if you'll bring some eggs."

"I've got plenty," she said. They were quiet looking out at the immense unfolding of another day in paradise. "Did you know that crocuses are what they make saffron from?" she asked. "Those bright red-orange threads you get when you buy saffron are actually the stigma, the female portion of the plant."

"Why's it so expensive?" he asked.

"It takes a lot of them, I guess," she said.

"Speaking of the female parts of plants, when will we get started growing pot?"

"Soon. We'll start sprouting seeds. I'll show you."

They didn't talk much. Up here, above houses and cars and shopping lists, it was as if they were on a cloud in heaven. The only sound was the wind and the trilling of a mourning dove in the distance. Lady Jessica and Caliber were running after squirrels in a frenzy of excitement. A large bird launched from the top of a tall tree and sailed over them to get a better look.

"I'm hoping we've seen the last of the cold weather," Meera said. "I asked Sam Bosse, the local sheep shearer, to come up soon and give Honey Lamb her annual haircut. She's driving me crazy. Her rear end is completely matted in sheep poop. I had to use a metal rake to untangle it enough for her to be able to shit. Poor thing."

Sasha smiled, but said nothing. Then, remembering, said, "Caliber treed a bear last night."

"How big was it?"

"Bigger than me, but not full grown yet. By the way, I'm almost finished *Dune*. I can't stop thinking about it. The quote you gave me about fear has become my religion. Can't wait to read *Dune Messiah*. Have you read it yet?"

"Of course, we all have."

"We?"

"All the Bene Gesserit."

"Of course." He paused. "I'll bring it down to you when I'm done."

"No need. Keep it with you. If I need it, I'll know where it is."

They were quiet again. The sound of their voices was an intrusion on the crystal silence. Finally, Sasha spoke. "This is like church here. This spot feels like holy ground. I think I'd like to be buried here. I read a poem last night by Hyemeyohsts Storm, the Native American guy who wrote *Seven Arrows*. He described how he wanted to be laid out on the ground after he died, rather than be buried, and let insects and birds and animals feed from his body. I'd like to do the same, right here."

Meera smiled and nodded. "A perfect place. If I live longer than you, I'll carry you up here and say a prayer." She paused a moment. "I loved the story of Jumping Mouse. *Seven Arrows* is a sacred book. I was told by some Indian activist friends that it was quite controversial. Some of the young bloods thought it gave away too many secrets to white folks."

"I can see that," he said. "There's a lot of wisdom in that book. But I think Storm believes it's their role now to enlighten us honkies. We obviously need it." He paused for a moment, not sure whether to ask this. "Tell me how you became a leftist, Meer."

A gust of wind came down from the mountain above them. She sat silently for a moment in thought, looking out at the horizon, before she told him her story. "I grew up in a rather conservative, secular family in Baltimore. My parents were nominally Christian, but I was raised without religion. When I was a freshman at the University of Maryland Law School, having graduated the semester before from Goucher College in

Baltimore, I took a part-time job as a case worker in the welfare department. At orientation, I was the only white girl in a room of mostly black women and one very handsome, charismatic young black man named Tyrone Cleveland. I somehow got in an argument with him about the Kennedy assassination. 'Of course Lee Harvey Oswald was a lone assassin,' I said. 'The Warren Report proved that. If you can't trust the Chief Justice of the Supreme Court, whom can you trust?'"

"All those black women roared with laughter. What did I know. I was just a dumb, naive white girl from the suburbs. Tyrone was married to a classmate of mine, Rebecca Cleveland, a year ahead of me at law school, whom I knew of but had never met. Our little debate on the Kennedy assassination turned out to be the first act in my political, sexual and cultural awakening. After orientation we had some lunch at a Jewish delicatessen and then I invited him up to my apartment. Both of my roommates were out. We smoked some pot and made love like I had never done before. The next day his wife came up to me at school and told me she was cool with my having an affair with her husband." Meera laughed, shaking her head. "This was the Sixties, after all. Rebecca invited me over to their house for dinner. It was all very open, very civilized. I learned that Rebecca was having her own affair with a white guy named Tom."

"I practically lived at their house in Cherry Hill, in the black ghetto, the rest of the year. Tyrone and Rebecca introduced me to the speeches and autobiography of Malcolm X, had me read dozens of books about the Vietnam War and everything I could get my hands on about colonialism. I read Chomsky and Franz Fannon, Wilfred Burchett and I.F. Stone, Marcuse and Marx. I got real involved in the antiwar movement in Baltimore. I also took my first acid trip at a Janis Joplin concert. I wasn't the same afterwards. I was a rebel with a cause. I felt I had been lied to my whole life and finally was waking up."

She stopped for a moment. Sasha could tell she was considering how much to share with him. "How did your family deal with all this?" he asked.

Meera laughed. "Oh, they were very concerned, but they never stopped loving me. First generation immigrants are never completely sure of their security and they worried that I'd bring unwanted attention to our family."

"Did you?"

"Not then," she said. "But I was definitely on the FBI's radar, especially after I made some derogatory remarks on TV about President Johnson."

"What happened with you and Tyrone?"

"Well, Rebecca got pregnant. At first, they weren't sure whether the baby was Tyrone's or Tom's, but they determined it was Tyrone's. The scare, though, made us all realize the political danger our relationship posed for them both. They were leaders in the Black Power movement in Baltimore. Tyrone's parents owned the largest African-American newspaper. It would be a huge scandal for them to be found having relationships with a couple of white folks. We all knew we had to end the affairs. It was very painful. I was in over my head and I knew it. I dropped out of law school. I didn't know what I would do. Then Rebecca introduced me to Tom McDowell, her boyfriend."

"What was he like?"

"Tom was a shop steward for the International Typographical Union. The ITU local was one of the only craft unions in Baltimore to actively support the anti-war movement and it had paid for Tom to go to Mississippi with the Student Non-Violent Coordinating Committee to register blacks to vote. He was a hardened and sophisticated organizer who commanded the respect of everyone around him and he was the first self-identified Marxist I had met. He was Irish, wore his long brown hair in a ponytail. He was tall and muscular with a nose that looked like it had been badly broken. He spoke in a constant stream of profanities with a slight Irish brogue. Rebecca took me aside to suggest that maybe someday I would get together with Tom."

Meera stopped there. She seemed disturbed to reveal some of these memories. They were quiet. The dogs came running up to them, tongues hanging from their mouths. "Let's stop there for now," said Meera. "I promised Jeffrey I would look after some things at his house while he was away."

"Away? I thought he never left here."

"I'm real worried about him. He drove down to San Francisco for some tests. That's all I know."

Chapter 17

The faucet wheezed, coughed and burped and, with a final pop, surrendered its water. Brown at first, it soon cleared. Sasha put on a pot to boil for coffee. He opened the firebox and blew on the kindling. He used a copy of Mother Jones magazine to fan the flames. Soon it was roaring. The morning was decidedly warmer. He went out on his deck in a T-shirt and played Keith Jarrett's Koln Concert on his cassette recorder as he began a set of tai chi. He found it hard to concentrate. His mind was on the conversation he had just had with Meera. He tried following his leading hand, then focused on exhaling and inhaling in time with each movement and slowed to match the tempo of Jarrett's improvisational soliloquy. He finished just as one could hear the pianist in the background of the tape softly moaning in ecstasy.

Meera came up at that moment bearing a basket of eggs. "They're still warm," she said. She handed him the basket, which also had a napkin folded around a loaf of coffee cake. "What's with the cables?" she asked, pointing to his truck, its hood open with two cables leading from the battery to the yurt.

"The feed store had some twelve-volt lights for sale. When I come home I attach some jumper cables and I can run a reading light and a cassette player off it. I don't think it will drain the battery before I drive somewhere and recharge it. If it does, I'm pointed downhill, so it should be easy to jumpstart."

"Very impressive," she nodded.

"I hate fluorescent lights, but electricity sure beats kerosene lamps for reading," he added. "I was going blind with them." He turned off his cassette player and carried the basket inside. Lady Jessica laid down next to Caliber on the rug in front of the fireplace. They both were tired from chasing squirrels. "That was fun this morning, Meera. I'm really drawn to that spot. The first time I walked up there, there was a herd of thirty or more deer and the view is so beautiful."

"Yea. How're your feet?" she asked. "I noticed you were bleeding."

He looked down at his feet. There was blood on the side of his right foot. He shrugged. "I guess they're fine. I didn't even notice."

"That's the point, I suppose," said Meera.

He cracked four eggs into a bowl. "I've never seen yolks so rich looking, so orange," he said.

"I'll have to tell the girls that. They'll be proud," she said.

"I've been wondering whether I should raise chickens myself. It would make me feel more self-sufficient."

"If Armageddon happens, you'll at least have all the protein you need," she quipped. "And they will keep you laughing. There's nothing funnier."

"So, what would I need to do?"

"Well, first off, you'll need to build a chicken coop. Have you ever built anything before?"

"I once build a diorama for a sixth-grade history project, but that's about the extent of my carpentry experience."

"Don't worry. It's easy and Bruce will help you. We've still got plenty of plywood around and maybe enough shingles and roofing paper, too. This could be fun," she said.

"What about chickens?"

"It just so happens that I heard Dolly yesterday, a woman I know in Alderpoint, saying she had some pullets she wanted to sell."

"What kind of chicken is that?

"It's just a word for a young hen. It takes about six months for a chicken to start laying. Dolly's pullets are already four or five months old, so you could be getting eggs as soon as March. If you wait to get baby chicks, you won't get any eggs until the fall. Dolly'll only want five or ten dollars for each of hers, I should think. She's got Araucanas and Rhodies and Barred Rocks. I'll help you figure that all out. Next time you go into Garberville, I'll come with you and we can get the lumber and feeders, waterers and hen scratch."

Sasha was elated. "I'm psyched," he said. "Will Caliber be a problem?"

"No, he's used to being around my hens."

"What about roosters?"

"You only need them if you want to make babies. But they're mean and they'll terrorize your brood and keep you up at night with their incessant crowing."

"Guys can be a problem. Sounds like they need some gender sensitivity training," he said.

"True, but girls are such gossips and they're so vain. They've got their own issues."

Sasha put chopped onions, red peppers and mushrooms into a pan of sizzling butter, as they talked. He poured boiling water over coffee grounds in a Melitta coffee filter. As he stirred the vegetables, he returned to their earlier conversation on the mountain.

"What was it like for you having that affair with a married black man? How did your family react?" he asked.

"Oh, they never knew about it, I don't think. But they could see how much I had changed and it freaked them out. I pretty much lost all my friends then, too. It's not that they abandoned me so much as I had nothing more in common with them. We fought about civil rights and the war and such and I just felt more and more alienated from them. It was a very lonely time for me. I had no one I could talk to except Tyrone and Rebecca. I finally confided in one of my old girlfriends who had become a born-again hippy and she thought it was 'so cooool,'" she mocked. "After Rebecca got pregnant, I had a little scare of my own. There's nothing like a missed period to sharpen the mind, I say. It was all too much. I felt I had lost my family, my friends and my country and now Rebecca and Tyrone would have to separate from me, too. I finally just dropped out, of law school and everything else. I had a little savings, enough to travel a bit, so I went to live in the south of France and then Morocco for a while. By the time I got back, the shit had really hit the fan in America."

She stopped there and watched as Sasha poured in the beaten eggs and added cheddar cheese, then expertly formed a perfect omelet. "Voila!" he exclaimed, as he flipped it over.

"Julia Child would be proud of you, Sash," she said. "Your turn now. Tell me how you were politicized," she asked.

They sat down at the table. He poured them coffee and laid out the cake on a plate. "It was totally different for me than it was for you. I didn't have a conversion experience like you did. I grew up in a family that already had no illusions about this country. The idea of 'American exceptionalism' was a joke to them. The Vietnam War simply confirmed their beliefs. Same with civil rights. My parents were too cynical to get involved, but they were totally sympathetic. They already experienced how a country could turn against a minority. Their survival strategy was just to keep their heads down."

"And you?" she asked.

"Me? To this day, I'm not sure whether I stayed away from being an activist because of fear—probably not—or because I had some notion that I could best contribute by teaching the lessons of history. I thought I understood the contradictions that led Communists the world over to eat their own. The anti-war and civil rights movements were based too much on emotions and lacked a unifying analysis. Even non-violence.

That was a tactical device, but it wasn't a strategy. I had illusions that I might bring some clarity as things developed."

"Did you?"

"No, not at all. I ended up being a bourgeois academic teaching a bunch of bored, innocent young white kids."

"You and Tom would have clashed," she said.

"Tell me about him."

"Tom was a man of action. Action and more action. He was always the first person to charge police lines at a demonstration. The world was all black and white for him. He called himself a Marxist, but he really was more of an anarchist. He was a very romantic character, I suppose. He almost got himself killed down South working with SNCC; but they eventually kept their distance from him, afraid he might be a provocateur. When I got back from Morocco, I looked him up. Turns out he was in jail for attacking police during the Democratic National Convention in Chicago. I helped bail him out."

"Did you ever get together with him, like Rebecca said?"

"I married him."

Sasha's mouth dropped open and then a smile spread across his face. "How amazing! You each married the lover of your lover's spouse. You can't make stuff like that up." Meera didn't say anything. Sasha continued. "I've often wished I were more like Tom," he said. "I admire people like that, moved to act on their convictions. I'm too self-critical I guess. I'm always seeing the bigger picture, the things that can go wrong, to ever be a leader like that. If Tom saw the world in black and white,

I see it all in greys. Reason can only carry you so far, though. Sometimes you need blind passion to change things."

He could see Meera looking at him differently, her head cocked, taking the measure of him again. "But, Sasha, you should know, as well as anyone, how ultimately self-destructive such a passionate belief in yourself and your cause can be. I watched it happen with him, with us. Neither of us believed we could reform the system. Capitalism couldn't be overthrown except by force. Black revolutionaries were leading the way, but Tom believed that the only possibility of building a revolutionary movement in America was to radicalize the white working class. He saw himself as a leader in building a multiracial, class-conscious revolution," she said.

"The American Lenin," said Sasha.

"Yes, something like that."

They were silent for a minute. "More coffee?" he asked. Meera nodded. He got up and made more coffee and poured them both some. "Where were you in all this?" he asked.

Meera sipped her coffee and then said, "I was supportive up to a point. We shared the same goal and the same analysis, but we constantly differed about the need for violence. I wasn't a pacifist or anything, far from it; but I believed it was dangerously premature to talk about it. Violence would only keep us from ever winning the support of the masses. But Tom believed we had to use violence to show the system was vulnerable. We argued constantly. Tom thought it was legitimate to attack property, so long as we were careful not to harm anyone. He got involved with an underground cell of radicals who had broken from the Weather Underground and were planning to blow up some PG&E electricity towers. I was vehemently opposed to them. I wanted no part in it. I told him I would leave him, if he didn't stop. I meant it."

"Did you?"

Meera's face contracted in pain. She was on the verge of crying. "That's another story," she said. "I'm surprised that I've told you this much. But it feels really good to have a friend I can talk to. Jeffrey knows about all this, but we rarely mention it anymore. It's like we're living in a parallel universe. I'm glad we talked."

Sasha wanted to hold her in his arms, but he didn't move. Instead, he asked, "What kind of chickens should I get?"

Chapter 18

The sound of moaning woke Sasha up, his own, he quickly realized. He had been dreaming of Darlene, making love with her in the tall grass by the buckeye tree. He reached down and felt the sticky goop on his legs and on the sheet. "Fuck!" he cried out loud. He wondered when he had last done that. Probably around age 13, he thought. He would have to go to town now for sure to do his laundry. He needed to go anyway, he knew. His propane was running low. The trip would take up half the day, but the drive over the mountain was always an epiphany, breathtakingly beautiful, and there would be a milkshake and other treats when he got there.

It was still dark, but Sasha got out of bed anyway. It would take an hour or two to heat up enough water for a shower. Besides, "a night without sleep is a day gained," he recalled some Buddhist saying. The wicker basket where he kept his kindling was empty and he was low on newspapers, too. He walked outside naked with a flashlight and picked up some madrone branches just behind his yurt. If they bent without snapping, they were too green; he'd drop them in search of some drier, more seasoned kindling. There was nothing like a good supply of kindling to make one feel secure, he thought. He promised himself to collect a basketful before the day was out. It was very chilly, but certainly warmer than it had been. The sky overhead was radiant with stars. They twinkled more up here.

When he got back inside, he covered himself with a blanket, started a fire in the cook stove and ground some coffee beans with an old-fashioned hand grinder. He dressed, cleaned the soot off all the lanterns in the house with a paper towel, trimmed the wicks and lit the lamps. The soft light filled the round room. He tried to remember his dream, to no avail, but the thought of Darlene started to arouse him again. *I am alone in the Garden of Eden*, he thought, *but without an Eve*. He sat in his one comfortable chair and turned on his new fluorescent reading light. He was almost through Rodale's 900-page *Encyclopedia of Organic Composting*, which he had borrowed from Meera. Anxious to start building a composting pile of his own, he looked forward to getting an early start on the day.

His morning routine had become a comforting ritual: starting a fire in the cook stove, making coffee, doing a set of tai chi to the music of the Koln Concert. By the time he finished his coffee this morning, the sky was starting to lighten. He could almost feel the earth yawn and stretch its limbs, the woods come to life. The Rodale book chronicled the history of composting, each chapter describing the next iteration of an ever more efficient design. By the end, the authors touted a seemingly miraculous alchemical process that could turn shit into loamy, sweet-smelling compost in just ten days. Sasha was determined to replicate this feat. To that end, he set out early, while the sun had just peaked on the horizon, with his cache of twenty burlap coffee bags to harvest enough cow poop to help fire his compost pile.

He parked Tuffy by the side of the road next to a large open pasture where he had seen a herd of cows grazing a few days before. And there, scattered amongst the chewed and matted grass were nuggets of the cow pies that Carl had talked about. As he approached, like a miner discovering an open vein of gold, he stepped on a fresh pie, which squooshed warm and wet between his naked toes. Disgusted, he would not be deterred. Regrettably, though, most of the pies in this field of dreams were similarly too fresh. He tried picking up one that had greyed and crusted on top, but it turned to mush in his hands. Still, he was determined. He felt called by some higher power. Further up the pasture, he came across new deposits that were undoubtedly older with fresh grass shoots growing through them. But these disintegrated into dust as he lifted them.

Finally, he found the mother lode, a football field-sized pasture covered in random plops of poop that were neither too fresh nor too old, firm but nutritious. Priding himself on his discernment, Sasha began filling sack after sack with these organic Frisbee-like discs. By the time the sun had passed overhead and the day lay awake in its full glory, Sasha had managed to fill all twenty burlap bags and dragged them back to the road, flinging them triumphantly onto the bed of his truck. He was exhausted. *If only Larry could see me now*, he thought. Dr. Alexander Simonov, Associate Professor of Rus-

David Hoffman

sian History, author of *Bukharin's Theory of Equilibrium*, his hands and bare feet covered in shit, had graduated.

When he got back to his house, he found Charles at the table thumbing through the composting book, smoking a joint.

"Where've you been, bro?" asked Charles. "I saw your truck was gone, but there was a fire in the stove. Figured you'd be back soon. I kept it going, helped myself to some coffee." He handed the joint to Sasha. "Holy crap, man, you smell like shit."

"I know," said Sasha. "I've been collecting cow pies. I'm going to make an enormous compost pile to plant my crop in. I think I can do it in ten days." He turned to the last chapter and showed it to Charles. "I've got a huge pile of elephant shit, too, that I brought up from the zoo in San Francisco."

Charles looked at him skeptically. "Why elephant dung?" he asked.

"Why not? I figure that would make some enormous fucking pot."

Charles shook his head. "Actually, the smaller the animal, the more concentrated the protein. I mean, the elephant dung will work fine, but ounce for ounce, ant shit is way more potent."

Sasha felt deflated, but laughed at himself. "Well, according to this book, turning shit into compost will increase the strength of the fertilizer eight times, so maybe it will all equal out."

"If you want, I can show you where you can get some bat shit," said Charles, smiling, his mouth full of missing teeth. "You can buy guano at the feed store for $90 a bag. But I know where there's a cave near the bridge down by Little Dobbyn Creek. Nobody knows about it but me. I'd be happy to share

130

it with you. It's freaky in there, but there's tons of the stuff. I've thought of selling it to the feed store, but what the fuck. They get theirs from Belize. You can get all you can carry by scraping it from the floor of this cave."

Sasha was impressed, not just by what Charles knew, but his generosity as well. "Thank you. I'd really appreciate that. I'd be happy to share some of my compost with you when it's ready, maybe just two weeks or less from now."

Charles handed him a baby food jar with seeds in it. "Here's that purple triple cross, I was telling you about. That's what we're smoking now."

Indeed, it was some of the most potent pot, Sasha had ever smoked. "Thanks. This stuff is really, really strong," he said and then asked, "Hey bro, have you had anything to eat yet?"

Charles shook his head. "I stayed at Bruce and Kimmy's last night. They're coming back in a week or so. I had some of Meer's eggs this morning. She made me an omelet, so I'm good. But thanks." He thought for a bit, then said, "You know, you can get all the chicken and horse shit you want for free. People in Alderpoint are more'n happy to trade you for cleaning out their coops or their horse stalls. I do that for my own grow. Chicken shit has some strong nitrogen. You got to be careful not to use it straight or it'll burn the plants' roots. But composting it will take the burn out for sure. Me, I think pot likes horse shit the most. Nelly Mauchamp's always asking me to clean out her horse stalls. We could go there tomorrow, if you want."

131

"I'd love that. I'm heading into Garberville today. You want to come along?" asked Sasha.

"I'd love to. Meera said you might be going. That's why I stopped by, hoping you were headed to town. I think she'd like to come with us, too, if you were." He sniffed the air. "You might want to shower first, though."

Chapter 19

Caliber barked and stood by the door wagging his tail. It was then that Sasha heard the sound of a car coming up the road. He heard it trail off before it reached his drive. *Must be Jeffrey coming back*, he thought. The sunset had faded, but there was still some light left in the sky. He decided to walk down to Jeffrey's house in case he needed any help. He grabbed his jacket and a flashlight. Caliber led the way. Meera arrived at the same time he did, her face grey.

Jeffrey's house was a simple one-story, one-bedroom structure sitting on concrete blocks. It was only partially sided, as if it had been interrupted in its construction. A simple brick chimney rose from the rear. Three wood steps led to an aluminum screen door. "Come in," Jeffrey called out to them. Meera and Sasha entered into a cozy living room filled with upholstered couches. Jeffrey had turned on the propane heater and the room was already warm. There was a fireplace, but it hadn't been used in some years. Everything spoke function over form.

"I'm in the kitchen, make yourselves at home. Would you like some tea?" he asked.

Meera shook her head.

"No, we're good," Sasha answered for them both.

Jeffrey emerged carrying a tray with tea pot, honey and a saucer. He was wearing the same tan sweater he always wore, a pair of grey sweat pants and black slippers. "Please," he said, gesturing for them to sit.

Meera looked sternly at him. As he shuffled to his favorite chair and struggled to let himself down, the air seemed to come out of him. "Ah, it feels so good to be home," he sighed.

Sasha said nothing while Meera gave Jeffrey her "let's cut the bullshit" stare. "So?" she asked.

Jeffrey looked at her, then at Sasha and back at her again. "It's true," he said. "I am dying."

Meera's eyes swelled with tears. She stood up and went to him, bent to her knees and cradled him in her arms. He patted her back.

"How long?" Sasha asked, breaking the shrouded silence.

Jeffrey smiled, "More than an hour and less than a month, or maybe two. The cancer I apparently had in my colon has spread throughout my body. There's nothing they can do. Death will win. It always does."

"Are you comfortable?" Sasha asked.

Jeffrey laughed out loud. "That's what the nurse asked me. I said I had plenty of savings."

Meera got up, wiped her eyes on her sleeve, and sat back on the couch next to Sasha. "What's the prognosis, Jeff? What can you expect?"

"Dr. Bergman gave me some pills for pain, but I'd really like to stay as conscious as I can throughout this, right to the end. It's my last chance to experience something like this and I don't want to miss any of it. It helps to know that death will bring relief no matter how hard the ordeal. In any case, as Peter Pan said, 'Dying is an awful big adventure.'"

Sasha wondered how he'd handle his own dying. "Are you afraid?" he heard himself say.

"No, not at all. What's to be afraid of? I don't look forward to the dying part, but death I can welcome. I'm old. I've lived a long life. Imagine if we were immortal. Now that would be something to fear. Death absolves us all. It's evolution's divine forgiveness."

"I suppose so," said Sasha. "Is there anything we can we do for you?"

Jeffrey considered this. "For the moment, I can cook for myself. You could bring in the groceries before you leave, though. I realized I left them in the car. But just check in on me from time to time. I'm sure I'll need help with something." He turned to Meera. "Just keep me well supplied with your pot. That will be my medicine of choice."

"You know, you could move in with me. I've got plenty of room," said Sasha, surprising himself. "I would enjoy the company and I'd learn a lot." He could see that Meera and Jeffrey were impressed.

"That's very kind, Sasha, but not at all necessary. I don't want to be a burden for anyone and I know how difficult it can be caring for someone dying. I did that for my mother and for one of my sisters."

"How long have you known about this? asked Meera.

"I didn't know for sure, but there was blood in my stool and it hurt when I coughed. I debated whether to even go see Dr. Bergman, a long-time patient of mine and a friend. I knew I wasn't willing to go through any big intervention, but I needed to know how much time I could expect, to make plans." He paused for a moment, poured himself some tea and added a spoonful of honey before continuing. "I couldn't figure out how to dispose of my body. I didn't want to do anything that might compromise any of you. I wish we could just dig a hole around here and have you turn me into a worm farm. But I worried that somewhere down the road it might get you into trouble. Imagine if the cops busted you for pot and discovered a dead body. So, I arranged to be cremated. You'll have to do me one last favor and drive my body to Fortuna. Dr. Bergman will sign the death certificate and any paperwork." Meera and Sasha nodded their heads and shrugged. It all seemed so surreal.

"Oh, yes. And one more thing. I spoke to Judge Wallace, Andy Wallace. I told him what was happening with me and asked if I could buy this forty acres we're all living on from him. We agreed on a price. I stopped by my friend Joe Connally's office in San Francisco, my old lawyer, and he's arranging all the paperwork. I'm giving the land to you, Miriam. I thought of having you and Bruce own it together, but partnerships have a way of getting complicated. Just promise me you'll always allow Bruce to live here, if he wants."

Meera's tears now flowed freely. Sasha put his arms around her and held her close. The warmth and closeness of her was a carnal revelation, a reminder of what was missing in his life. But the emotional bond was even stronger, a ritual sharing, a kind of sacrament. His own eyes teared. He looked at Jeffrey who nodded. When Sasha released her, she went over to the old man and gripped him by his shoulders, then kissed him repeatedly on his face and his bald head, thanking him and telling him how much she loved him. It was only then that Jeffrey also cried.

When she sat back on the couch, Jeffrey said, "It's all so interesting, what you think of. I find myself having conversations with my mother, something I never do. Her name was also Miriam. Odd, isn't it? You would have liked her. She was all fire and light, a dancer, also like you. After I saw Dr. Bergman, I had a strange compulsion to drive over to Oakland to visit her grave, something I hadn't done since she was buried. I managed to find the cemetery, on a hill between an abandoned sheet metal factory and a row of dilapidated row houses, but for the life of me I couldn't locate her grave. It was very disconcerting. I sat in my car and wept, for all those souls that had gone before me. Now it was my turn."

Meera and Sasha listened, but said nothing. Jeffrey continued, "After that, I felt much better. On the drive up here, I thought about Mary almost constantly. I don't think I really understood the true tragedy of her disease until that drive. When you know there's no future, memories are all that's left of you. What can it be like when you lose those memories?

They're really all we have. What is the self anyway? Who is it that dies? We're just stories. I am the sum total of all my stories. I remember Mary telling me, 'You know who I am, but I don't know who I am.' It is so sad to realize these memories will die with you. That's ultimately what we grieve."

He wiped his eyes with his napkin. "Are you sure I can't get you any tea?" he asked.

They nodded, then Sasha asked, "When you think back now over your life, do you have any regrets. Would you do anything differently?"

Jeffrey smiled. "There's an old Yiddish proverb: 'A man is not old until his regrets take the place of his dreams,' but I don't have any regrets. Strangely, I still feel very young. I've had a great life. There's nothing I would change." He thought about that a moment. "Well, maybe learn the piano. My mother played. I grew up with a piano in the house, but I never learned to play. I think that would bring me a great deal of solace now."

They could see that he was getting tired. "We'll see you in the morning. You must be exhausted after all you've gone through and that long drive," Meera said, standing. "There's much to talk about." Sasha stood as well.

"Oh, Meera, one last thing," Jeffrey said. "I have news of Tom."

Meera put on her jacket and didn't say anything.

When they stepped outside, it was already dark. Meera took Sasha's arm. "I forgot my flashlight. Would you mind walking me home?"

Chapter 20

Sasha stopped to watch a pair of quail nervously trotting up the path. Hints of spring were everywhere: pink quince here and there and small green buds forming on the tips of trees. In no time, the land would flip from black and white to color. He breathed in the odor of the rich earth and the manure he was shoveling into a giant mound, felt the strength of his body and the warm sun on his arms. Meera walked up to the gate of the well-fenced garden that Carl had left him, sipping coffee from a mug.

"You're just in time to witness a miracle," Sasha said.

"I can see that," she laughed. "What's the chicken wire for?" A roll of chicken wire stuck out on either end of the pile and another stood upright from its center.

"It works as a bellows and chimney," he said.

"That chimney's pretty high. How big is this compost pile going to be?"

"As high as I can make it, six feet at least, but it should shrink to about four or five when it's ready." He paused before adding, "In just ten days, which is the world record." He showed her the mounds of elephant dung, the twenty bags of cow pies, the pile of horse shit and chicken manure he and Charles had cleaned from Nelly Mauchamp's farm and, most proudly, a wheel barrow full of freshly harvested bat guano. There was also an enormous mountain of mulch and leaves he had gathered. "The trick, I think, is having the right proportions, three-parts green matter to one-part shit, turning it from time to time and keeping it just moist enough, like a wrung-out sponge."

"Astonishing," she said. "Where did all this beautiful mulch come from?"

"I dug it from around the base of trees near here. Charles showed me."

"Sounds like you and Charles have become buds."

"We have. I'm trading him some of the finished compost for all his help."

Meera shook her head in amazement. "You are quite the overachiever, Sash, aren't you?"

"I suppose so. I like scale. I like the challenge. It's much more satisfying working with my body instead of my head." Sasha reached into the pocket of his cut-off sweat pants and pulled out a baggie of cannabis seeds. "Look at this. Check out what else Charles gave me."

Meera examined them. "They look really good, really full. I like how large they are. Here, I brought you some of mine, too, and some peat moss plugs. You can start sprouting these today, if you want. I started mine this morning."

"Thanks. Can you show me what to do? I can finish this later."

As they left the garden, Meera pointed out a bed of asparagus starting to come up like soldiers. "You've got lots of perennials that will show themselves soon. They'll love some of your compost," she said. "You'll have a ton of strawberries." They closed the gate and walked up to the yurt and went inside. There was still a fire going in the cook stove. Sasha put on a pot for tea. They sat at the table.

Meera spread Charles' and her seeds on two flat plates. "You can sort of guess which are most viable by looking at the seeds." She held up a nice round one and pushed aside a few that looked compromised. "Of course, you can never tell for sure." She handed him a bag of small two-inch peat moss plugs. "We'll plant the seeds in these after they've sprouted." She went to the sink and soaked some paper towels in warm water and placed them on two plates. "Here, put your seeds on these and cover them with more wet towels. Keep track of which are from Charles and which from me. Most importantly, don't let your towels dry out. Keep misting them so they stay nice and moist. I like to keep mine in a warm place near the stove. In a day or two they should start to sprout."

Sasha felt his heart beat with excitement. This is the day he'd been waiting for. He had made it through the winter, experiencing weeks on end by himself, taught himself the basic rudiments of living in the woods and was finally ready to start his crop. He was proud of the compost pile he was making and eager to get started. "Sometimes I feel like a seed myself, small and fragile but on the verge of growing."

"You've grown a lot already," said Meera. "When you arrived with that truck full of elephant shit, I wasn't sure you'd make it. I had to wonder. But I was much like you when I came up here, a city girl. I had a lot of support from Jeffrey and Bruce, though. I couldn't have done it without them. But you've mostly had on the job training. I've noticed you've grown physically, too. Your shoulders are broader and your gait is more athletic."

Sasha felt himself blush. "Thanks," he said. He looked at Meera's tall and slender body. She had a long neck, like many French women, he'd seen, but her eyes were definitely more exotic, Middle Eastern, though he had never really known other women from that area. She held herself straight like a model. He wondered how she'd look in more feminine attire.

"Did you happen to see Jeffrey this morning?" he asked.

"I stopped by there before I came down here, but he was sleeping."

"I've noticed he's sleeping more," said Sasha. "He seems to diminish a little each day. We've had some really good conversations, though. I'm learning a lot from him. It's made me think I should probably spend more time with my parents. They're getting old and I feel like there's so much about my family that I don't know. After harvest, I may go back East and spend some real time with them." He paused a moment. "What about your parents, Meer?"

Meera's face seemed to wilt. "I don't have any contact with them anymore."

Sasha expected her to clam up, as she usually did when she told the darker parts of her past, but she continued.

"My parents disowned me when Tom and I got married. Actually, we never officially were married, but we told our parents that we were. We were planning to disappear, to go underground, and we wanted to say our goodbyes. We knew we wouldn't be able to contact them after that, so we tried our best to assure them that we knew what we were doing and we were safe with each other. But, of course, we didn't have a clue what the future held for us. We told them we were going to Canada until the war ended in case the FBI came around, but we were actually headed to the Bay area. My parents were hysterical. I was never able to talk with them again."

There was a long minute of silence. Finally, Sasha asked, "What happened when the war ended?"

Sasha could see the muscles in her face tighten and her body tremble. She didn't cry, but it took effort not to. She would tell him in her own time, if she wanted. He shouldn't push her, he thought. She remained still, looking down, not speaking. But Sasha could see how hurt she was. He moved next to her and put his arms around her. It felt good to hold her so close, but her pain was palpable.

When she finally composed herself, she pulled away and said, "I hadn't planned to share any of this with you, for reasons you'll soon understand, but I know you too well now to keep secrets from you. We have the chance to be really good friends, Sash, but we can't if you only know the half of me."

She heard the kettle vibrating on the stove. "Can I have a cup of tea first, though?"

He got up and poured them each hot water in a mug and placed a silver tea strainer in hers. "Some honey?" he asked. She spooned some honey into her mug and stirred it slowly. After some moments, she continued her story. "Tom and I got deeply into the radical politics of San Francisco and the Bay area—Black Panthers, Weather Underground, you name it. We were intent on remaking ourselves, on exorcising all the myths and values we were taught growing up as middle-class Americans. It was a crazy time. We experimented with everything. For a while we lived in a commune where we all threw our clothes in a pile and whatever pair of pants you pulled out was who you slept with, man or woman. We did all kinds of drugs. We hated everything about the culture, the exploitation of children in Disney films, everything. And we argued, all the time, about tactics and strategies for the coming revolution. It was nuts."

"Tom had gone somewhere—he wouldn't even tell me—to get some training in explosives. I was violently opposed to doing anything like that. We fought constantly. Finally, I made up my mind to leave him and told him so." Meera paused and stared at her mug. A tear rolled down her cheek. She shook her head and then continued, "I had gone to Jeffrey's house, in fact—he was my therapist and we had become best friends. I told him I was leaving Tom and asked if I could stay at his apartment for a couple days until I decided where to go next. When I walked back to my place to get my suitcase, I heard a loud explosion. At first, I didn't think anything of it, but I soon saw black smoke rising from the direction of our apartment and there were lots of sirens converging and when I got there I saw that the entire house had been destroyed."

She looked up and made eye contact with Sasha, her eyes wet with tears. He held her hand. When he let go, she said, "Our neighbor, Celia, from downstairs was killed. I watched them take her body out in a gurney. I found out later on the news that Tom had been badly burned, but was alive. I was completely out of my mind, as you can imagine. I figured they would be looking for the woman who had been seen at the apartment with Tom. I knew Tom would never tell them about me, but one way or the other I was a wanted woman. I had to escape, had to disappear. I think the rest you know. Jeffrey saved me. Here I am."

After a minute or two Sasha asked, "What ended up happening to Tom?"

Meera managed a sardonic smile. "Up until a few days ago, I had absolutely no idea. I've religiously avoided the news. I haven't read a newspaper or listened to the radio since then. But Jeffrey told me he heard from his lawyer that Tom was in Soledad Prison and had become a Zen priest. Frankly, it made perfect sense to me."

Sasha let out a long sigh. So, she was not a widow, as he had assumed and her story did not yet have an ending, or so it seemed. He had spent his academic life trying to get into the heads of radicals and revolutionaries. Listening to her though, he realized he had not sufficiently understood their hearts. Did Meera still love Tom, he wondered? And, to his surprise, he realized that this question mattered a lot to him. For the first time, he saw the crack across the grain of her being and felt irresistibly drawn to her. But would she be available?

Chapter 21

Sasha didn't hear Bruce and Kimmy approach until they opened the garden gate, startling him.

"Hey bro, Whatcha up to?" asked Bruce.

"Turning shit into gold," laughed Sasha.

He put down his shovel and embraced them. "You guys look great," he said. He held his arm next to Kimmy's. "Quite a suntan. How was it? Where'd you go? I missed you."

They sat on an old railroad tie by the compost pile, passing a joint between them, while Bruce and Kimmy related stories of beaches and tequila, of hiking through a rainforest and getting lost in the mountains near Michoacan, of hitchhiking a ride on the back of a truck full of mangos and papayas and getting deathly sick on the way to Oaxaca.

"It all sounds great, but if you were to go back anywhere, where would you go?"

They looked at each other and smiled. "Yelapa," answered Kimmy. Bruce nodded in agreement. "There's no electricity. Imagine being here with warm weather and a beach."

"And a pie lady," added Bruce, "who comes around every morning with fresh baked pies in a basket balanced on her head, singing 'Chocolate, limon, coconut, vanilla,'" imitating her.

They had heard about Jeffrey's diagnosis when they ran into Meera on her way to town to buy him some groceries and refill his propane tank. She told them that he had asked her not to fill the tank too full, that he would die before it ran out and didn't want them to waste the money. "That is so Jeffrey," Bruce said.

"We've had some great talks about death and dying," said Sasha. "I was telling him about how I was making compost in ten days," he said, pointing to the pile in front of them "and he said we were all in a state of composting, of living and dying. He wished we could just compost his body and feed him to our plants and smoke him."

"Holy shit!" Bruce said, shaking his head.

"Yeah, literally," said Sasha.

"That would be some really fucked up pot," said Kimmy.

Sasha picked up a handful of compost and handed it to her. "Smell this. This is day 10."

She held it to her nose. It smelled sweet like freshly turned soil, not like manure. "This is like potting soil. What did you do?"

He explained what he had learned from the Rodale Encyclopedia, about keeping the pile aerated with just the right moisture, how the rolls of chicken wire worked, and about nitrogen-to-green matter ratios and all the different sources of shit he used. "Yesterday, it was steaming like a chimney and too hot to touch."

"Professor, you've come a long way," laughed Bruce. "This is impressive."

They left to go see Jeffrey. Sasha picked up his shovel and returned to his alchemy. But when Bruce got to the gate, he suddenly turned and said, "Oh, Sasha, I forgot. I picked up the mail in town. There's a letter for you, in care of Carl." He walked back and handed Sasha a lightweight, prepaid airmail envelope, the kind with blue stripes around the margins.

"Thanks." Sasha felt his heart rate spike when he saw the return address, "Bodi Dharma Commune," Ashland, Oregon. *Darlene, thank God.*

Dear Sash,

How are you? Thank you for your letter. I loved your descriptions of the people and the harvest trimming scene. And Caliber. And everything. It sounds like you've found your paradise.

Rolf has a grower friend in Honeydew. I think that's near you, if I understand right. His friend invited us to come trim for him in the Fall. It sounds like lots of fun and we can make good money in a short time. Maybe we could visit you, if we go there. It would be so great to see you. I often think of our fun times together. It kind of surprises me, actually, how often.

Life here is all hard work and hard play, though, honestly, we are too tired much of the time to play very much. But we did get to see Bruce Springsteen in Portland this weekend. It was definitely a "two-panty kind of night," as my Aunt Billie would say. But most days, we are up before dawn and don't usually stop till dark. We're building eight new cabins. There's a hundred-year old house that we've all been living in through the winter, all twenty-three of us. With Spring, many of us are moving into tents until the cabins are finished, including Rolfie and me. We're also building an enormous bio-energetic garden with raised beds and a large fenced-in area for chickens and goats. We expect to produce all the food we need. Our goal is to be 100% self-sufficient.

Living so closely with a group of people can be challenging sometimes, but we're becoming like a family. (Three of the women are pregnant.) Rolfie is our leader and we're all here because of him; but it's not always easy being the one who has to make the hard decisions. As for me, I am learning so much. I understand what you always said about wanting to grow, about challenging ourselves. Sounds like you're doing that in spades. So am I, I guess. Well, please write again. I loved hearing your stories and hope that I can see you in the Fall.

Hugs and Kisses,
Darlene

Sasha reread the letter three times. He noted she wrote "Maybe **we** could visit you" and later, "hope that **I** can see you in the Fall." He prayed she might come by herself. The thought of that made him intensely horny. And over and over he repeated to himself the sentence where she said how often she thinks of their fun times together. The thought of sharing this paradise with her, of making love in the sand on the beach in Alderpoint, in the grass up in the high meadows on Grizzly

Mountain or in his bed in front of the fireplace, drove him mad with desire. Would he look back on this letter, he wondered, as some sort of turning point in his life?

He continued to work all day in the garden, double digging the beds that Carl and Kimmy had started, putting a layer of fresh horse shit on the bottom to draw roots down with its heat. He dug a large, deep trench at the top of the garden that would get the first sun each day and layered it with manure, soil and compost. He planted sunflower seeds every two feet the length of the trench. Charles told him that the size of a hole would determine the breadth of the plant's root structure, so he dug deep and wide. The pot holes would be his priority, but he had big plans to plant tomatoes, corn and string beans, onions, garlic, beets, squashes and lots and lots of flowers. By the time his shadow was longer than his body, he was exhausted. He could feel his back tightening like a rubber band stretched to its limit. He plunged his shovel into the much-diminished compost, a flag of conquest, and went back to the yurt to take a cold shower.

He had inherited his mother's back trouble and was determined to prevent it from going out. There was simply too much work to be done in the weeks to come. Before he laid down, though, he checked on the pot seeds. Most of them had sprouted: tiny, fragile, pure white roots emerging from their seed pods into the daylight. So optimistic, so tender, so hungry for life, thought Sasha. He planted them individually into the Jiffy peat moss plugs, but Meera had pointed out that he was putting them in upside down. The fragile root should

151

point down, not the seed shell. Meera assured him it wouldn't be a problem, though. The new plant would be strong enough to right itself. And, indeed, in a couple days white roots emerged from the soil and summersaulted 180 degrees back into the dirt, lifting their fractured seed pods above them. He had more than enough sprouted seeds and began to plant two or three to a pellet. The ones that hadn't sprouted yet, probably never would, he concluded.

He lay on the floor with his legs propped up on a chair and dreamed of Darlene. He'd give anything for her to be there now, but part of him questioned whether she'd be a good match for him long-term, even if she were available. It was hard to imagine growing old with Darlene. He looked outside. The days were getting longer, but it would soon be getting dark. He had committed to looking in on Jeffrey and bringing him dinner. He struggled to his feet. His back was definitely becoming a problem. He grabbed the vegetable and tofu casserole he had made the night before and, with Caliber leading the way, walked to Jeffrey's house. There was an abundance of wildflowers along the path, mostly short, purple irises. Jeffrey had routinely scattered blood meal when he walked the path and nature had responded with a feast of colors.

He knocked lightly in case Jeffrey was sleeping, as he often did now, but there was a hearty "Come in" and he and Caliber entered. Jeffrey was sitting in his reading chair, a book beside him open on the floor. "Sasha, so good to see you. Take a seat."

It amazed him how Jeffrey remained so upbeat and mentally alert. "You're looking good, Jeffrey."

"Today's a good day," said Jeffrey. "I slept well. I've been down the last few days, a lot more pain when I breathe. I can tell the cancer's spread to my lungs. I can't even smoke pot anymore, but Meera's given me some peanut butter infused with it. I thought I'd run out of good days like this, so this was a surprise. On days like this, it's hard to believe I'm dying."

"Maybe the whole process is going to reverse itself and you'll start growing younger," said Sasha.

"Like Benjamin Button?"

"Exactly."

"It may be," said Jeffrey. "I actually woke up with a hard on this morning for the first time in years. You might be right."

Sasha smiled. "Jeffrey, you're an inspiration! I hope I'm as optimistic as you are when I'm your age, and as virile."

Jeffrey started to laugh, but had a coughing fit, instead. It brought tears to his eyes. "Optimistic, shmesimistic." Jeffrey waved his hands in a sign of dismissal. There's never a reason to feel optimistic or pessimistic, Sasha. When I first moved here, I experienced something like a religious epiphany. After a lifetime as a psychologist listening to other people's anxieties, I decided to put all my faith in reality. Worrying about the future or complaining about the past was just a waste of time, I realized. Worrying wouldn't make any difference. Things almost always turn out better than what we fear. So, I decided to put all my chips on reality. And I've never been disappointed."

Sasha was silent for a minute, then asked, "So, how are things right now?" For years to come, he would recall Jeffrey's spontaneous, unconstrained laugh.

"Perfect," Jeffrey exclaimed, his eyes luminous. "Simply perfect."

There followed another long coughing fit. Sasha got up and brought Jeffrey a glass of water.

"Thank you," said Jeffrey. "I don't mean to be so glib. Dying is hard. I do worry, for example, about how I'm going to manage when I can't get myself to the toilet anymore. Philosophically, I'm convinced that I'm more than just this body, but the damn thing sure demands a lot of my attention just now." He paused while he drank more water.

"Can I heat up this casserole for you?" asked Sasha.

Jeffrey shook his head, but said nothing. He closed his eyes. After several minutes, Sasha quietly got up, put some of the casserole in a bowl in the fridge and left.

Chapter 22

Spring dropped any pretense of being coy. Daffodils trumpeted its arrival. Trees burst in a dozen shades of green. Squirrels picnicked with abandon. Sasha literally dragged his body from bed and crawled to the deck to bathe in the suddenly hot sun. "You get what you fear," Jeffrey had told him once. He was right. If you believed you could manifest your thoughts, it worked for the bad as well as the good. "Fear is the mind-killer." When he had bent down earlier to gather some kindling, the muscles in his back closed shut like an iron vice. There was nothing he could do. The force was greater than he was. He could only surrender. The pain, though, hurt less than the helplessness. There was so much he needed to do.

Luckily, Meera came by every day. She brought him cereal in the morning and fed Caliber and started a fire for coffee. He had managed to crawl outside this morning before she arrived. Crawling was therapeutic, he had read somewhere. It felt like he was carrying a heavy safe on his back, but getting outside on this glorious day was worth the trouble. He was breathing hard when he propped himself against the wall of the yurt. At that height, Caliber couldn't resist licking him. He wished he had thought to bring a book and a pillow with him. It wasn't long, though, before Lady Jessica came scampering up the steps and made a beeline to cover his face with kisses before he managed to fight both dogs off. Meera was humming a song when she saw them attacking him and laughed.

"You have quite a fan club," she said. "Feeling any better?"

"I wish I could say I was, but I'm still in the grip of it. It feels like some medieval torture machine. But, I'm happy. Who wouldn't be on such a day?"

"I brought you some homemade muffins and some hot coffee in a thermos." She looked sternly at him. "You don't look very comfortable. Can I get you a pillow?"

"Oh, yes, please. Thank you. Could you also bring me the book by my bed?"

When she came back out, she settled next to him, sitting cross-legged. Neither of them said anything. They were serenaded by song birds. A cardinal sitting on a madrone branch belted out an aria that sounded, said Sasha, like he was singing "pretty girl, pretty girl." "He's singing for you," he told Meera. She blushed slightly. Neither of them had ever come on to the other. There was the slightest awkwardness, but it quickly passed.

"I watered your peat pods last night. I think it's time we moved your sprouts outside. They'll love the sun. I can help you transplant them into pots, if you'd like," she said.

"That'd be great," said Sasha. "We could do it together. It will be good to feel productive."

She brought out two trays of plump little seed pods and placed them on the deck next to him. Tender little two-leaf plants stood proudly in each pod. A few of them had two or three plants. Meera picked off the smaller of these. Sasha felt an impulse to stop her. These were his babies! She went to the garden and came back with a bag of potting soil and stacks of plastic planters. They worked in silence filling each planter with soil and placing the tiny pellets in them. It was a kind of meditation. He marveled at how often people up here were able to be quiet with one another, even when they weren't high. When they were finished he counted just over a hundred.

"Half of these will be males," she said, as she moved them off the deck to water them. "Once we sex them, we'll segregate the males far enough away that their pollen won't reach the girls. You should have more than enough females to fill your garden. Isn't it amazing to think that these tiny, fragile little things will grow to twice your height?"

"Yeah, and be worth more than their weight in gold, as you mentioned," he said.

They remained silent again. A wind came up sounding like snare drums through the new leaves. There were just a few white puff clouds drifting overhead. "Look," said Meera suddenly, pointing to the sky. A red-tailed hawk came dive-bombing from behind a cloud and trapped a young squirrel on the ground with its talons just a dozen yards from them. Meera jumped up and ran at it waving her hands and yelling for it to let the squirrel go. The magnificent bird took off peevishly with the squirrel still in its grip; but before it could get very high, the little rodent managed to squirm away, fell safely to earth and dashed off.

"My heroine!" shouted Sasha, wishing he could have run like that.

Meera came back beaming. "You might want to get a shotgun when you get your chickens," she said. "It can be real useful around here."

"Do you own one?" he asked.

"I don't. Lady Jessica is good at protecting the flock. She thinks they're hers. You can get by without a gun, but lots of folks around here will tell you you're crazy to live like this without one. By the way, Dolly's still holding those pullets for you. I told her you'd get them as soon as your back was better and were able to build a coop."

"Thanks. You can't imagine how ready I am. It's been 8 days now and I still can't stand or walk. It's very demoralizing."

"I can imagine you're getting frustrated," said Meera.

"I don't know what I would do without you, Meer. This is the busiest time of year and you're playing care giver to Jeffrey and me on top of everything else you've got to do."

"It's really my pleasure and not very hard. I'm making things for myself. It's just as easy to make a little extra. Besides, I love the opportunity to talk with both of you. Living by yourself can be very hard, especially when something like this happens. You learn to depend on the people around you. I love my solitude, but one can't live on solitude alone," she said.

Sasha thought about this. "Living in the city, we often take our friendships for granted. It's ironic that I felt lonelier living with my wife than I ever do living by myself up here."

Meera examined his face, looking to see any signs of sadness or regret, but there were none. She was exquisitely sensitive this way, he knew. He sometimes imagined she could read his mind.

"Tell me about your wife and how you broke up," she asked.

Sasha picked at his nails, wondering how he'd answer that. He smiled. "Well, Sarah was smart, pretty, not in a glamorous way, but attractive, I guess, and very serious, too serious. She was kind of a control freak, always critical. She'd come off in public as very nice, but when we were alone she'd have something bad to say about everyone. But mostly, she was hard on herself, and me especially. She was ruled by her superego, if you know what I mean. Neither of us had had much sexual experience, so when we started sleeping together, it just got habit forming, I guess. It wasn't like there were any good alternatives. It was just easier to keep going until one day we decided to make it formal." He stopped for a moment to watch Meera's expression.

"I hope I'm not being too hard on her. She had some great qualities, too. She could be very passionate about ideas. She had been seduced by Marxism. I think I had a big influence on her, disabusing her of any romantic attachment to its idealism, confronting her with the reality of life under Communism. She soon redirected her ideological fervor to radical feminism and became almost obsessed with a feminist critique of Marx and Marxism. I was much more nuanced about all this. I think the truth of things is much more likely to be found in the grey areas, in the contradictions themselves, in what's ironic, not the black and white world that attracted her. This is where we intersected, though. We had very similar interests around leftist politics and revolutionary thought, but we differed in our conclusions."

"Is this what broke you up?" asked Meera.

"Oh, no, not at all. I'm no Freudian, but I'd have to say the real issue was we weren't sexually compatible. She was very uptight." He paused for a moment, considering how explicit to be. "She was turned off by oral sex. She could go down on me, but I couldn't do the same for her. You can imagine how frustrated I became." *Could she?* he wondered. "Ironically, we both had secret affairs at the same time. Mine was with a librarian at the college and Sarah's was with a woman I had endlessly fantasized having a threesome with. I badly wanted Sarah to have a sexual relationship with her, never imagining she'd want to leave me. One has to be careful what one wishes for."

Meera slowly moved her head from side to side. "Amazing," she said. "I imagine she got over her fear of oral sex."

He noted how much he enjoyed talking with Meera so openly. He would not have been able to speak like this with Sarah.

"Tell me about the librarian," asked Meera.

"Her name was Darlene. She was entirely the opposite of Sarah, totally uninhibited. She loved sex. I could never smoke pot and make love with Sarah, but Darlene and I loved fucking stoned. She was utterly beautiful, great body, gorgeous strawberry blond hair down to her butt. Where Sarah was serious, Darlene was all play, like a child. Where Sarah was critical, Darlene only saw the good in everything, a real flower child. Darlene was into her senses and her body, where Sarah lived mainly in her head. Darlene taught me a lot, taught me how to play again."

"So, why didn't you go with her when Sarah left you?" asked Meera.

"Oh, she was engaged, more or less, infatuated with a lover who was like her guru. They had an open relationship. I knew she would be leaving to meet him, so it was always going to be a short-term affair. They met in an ashram in India and they're now living together in a spiritual community in Oregon. You may meet them this Fall. They might come out this way to trim pot in Honeydew and may visit us."

"Will I like her?" Meera asked.

For some reason this question brought up doubts he hadn't admitted to himself till that moment. *Would she seem too frivolous to Meera, too ungrounded? Would her spiritual talk sound like New Age gibberish?* "I don't know," he said, and the truth of that made him pause.

Chapter 23

He was late for class, hurrying along the stone walkway behind the lacrosse field. It was a dark, cloudy day, but strangely still. Students passed him on bicycles. He tried to run, but some force held him back, preventing him from making progress. His armpits were sweaty and he could feel a sense of panic rising from his gut. They would laugh at him, rushing into the lecture hall frazzled and late. And, to make matters worse, he had forgotten his notes or even what the subject was. When he finally arrived, the large oak doors were shut with a heavy metal chain across them. He pulled with both hands on the chain and frantically banged his fists to no avail. Finally, someone let him in, opening the doors from inside.

He fell forward into the classroom, tumbling to his knees, before he realized he was somewhere else. He found himself outdoors now in a field of tall grass. The sky had turned to a pale blue with lazy strands of clouds passing overhead. He heard the sound of horses approaching and turned to see a woman riding up to him bareback on a great chestnut mare holding the reins of a black stallion that trailed behind her.

The woman's face was painted in clown white with red and orange feathers around her eyes. When she smiled at him, he felt overcome with love, as if she were the beginning and end of all he had ever desired. She took off on her horse, smiling coquettishly at him. He raced after her on the stallion, ducking under tree branches, leaping over streams. When they stopped, he lifted her from her horse and laid on the grass next to her.

And then he woke up, disoriented, angry and alone. He wanted to smash things, but his infernal back remained locked in a vice. How could the universe tempt him with such love and snatch it away like that, he wondered? Who was she? Was it Darlene, Meera, or someone else? The dream meant something, he was sure. The feeling for this unknown woman was unlike anything he had ever felt in his waking life. Her absence was painful. Was his life so meaningless that he had never known such love? He had been married, but that was an act of convenience, more than anything else. There were moments with Darlene when he lost himself in desire. But even that didn't touch the full rapture he had just experienced, a love both carnal and divine.

He felt sapped of energy. He turned painfully and sat up. It was day ten or maybe eleven since his back went out. He was no longer sure. He thought of all the people in the world who were permanently paralyzed or disabled and took courage from them. *This too will pass*, he told himself. But there were bigger issues than his back problems, he knew, questions about his future. He had broken the patterns that had supported and reinforced a compromise with conventional life, had shown real courage in betting the safety of his past for the promise of an unknown future. It had been the right decision, he told himself. He had grown since he got here, in many ways. But the more self-confident and self-sufficient he had become, the more isolated he became. This was his paradox. How would he ever meet his soulmate on Grizzly Mountain?

He chided himself for letting himself get so down. If there was one guiding principle to his life, it was that happiness shouldn't depend on one's circumstance. What mattered is how you respond to the hand you are dealt. Fortune is fickle, he told himself, but an enlightened person could maintain a sense of equanimity no matter what the universe threw at you. Jeffrey got that. "Reality would be what it would be," he liked to say. It's easy to blame our unhappiness on fate, but doesn't that simply disempower us? He held his head in his hands. *How glib you are, Sasha*, he said to himself. *This enlightenment pep talk falls sadly short when it comes to finding a soulmate.* Yes, he was happy now living alone in nature, but could he do that indefinitely?

He fantasized what he'd do after harvest. If all went well, he'd have the money to travel for three months or so. He was in the prime of his life, physically in the best shape he'd ever been. Surely, he'd find some young French or Italian woman who'd want to share a life like his in the middle of such boundless beauty, growing plants for a living. His was the most romantic life imaginable, if only it could be shared. And what about Darlene? He doubted that she would ever leave her beloved Rolfie, but maybe if she were to experience his life here...

While these fantasies played in his head, lifting his spirits, a part of him could not ignore that a flesh and blood reality loomed just down the path. Meera had become the most intimate friend he'd ever known. They had shared the secret truths of their lives with each other. No one knew him as well as she did. But the trust between them was only possible, he knew, because he had respected the unspoken boundaries that protected her. Any hint of sexual desire would jeopardize this. She had nursed him while he lay immobilized in bed, read to him, cooked his meals. They talked endlessly about their dreams, their fears and hopes, and their spiritual beliefs. He was definitely attracted to her. How could he not be? She was elegant and classically beautiful, reminding him of faces he had seen on Etruscan urns. But he forced his mind to shut down whenever he thought of her this way. Besides, he knew she belonged to her husband, still alive, it appeared. She was not so much in mourning, as he first thought, but in waiting.

He longed to talk with her now. She embodied the situation that he had struggled with since he woke from his dream. Living with her chickens and Honey Lamb, Meera seemed perfectly content living alone. She never seemed lonely or needy or bored. He admired her independence. He wondered whether she ever felt sexually frustrated. She never showed any vulnerability and he realized that it was this self-sufficiency, more than anything else, that kept any romantic notions off the table.

It was just getting light outside. He felt a jolt of pain as he tried to shift to a more comfortable position. "The pain," he thought of it now. He gave it a color, red, and a shape, seeing if he could change them. The pain became purple and smaller, but it remained; and nothing, it seemed, could shake the iron vice that encased him. The most frustrating thing about his back troubles was that his body would not obey his mind. Muscles that usually did what he willed, were unresponsive. He struggled against the pain to crawl on all fours and, holding on to a chair, used all the power in his arms to right himself into a standing position. He stood like that for a minute catching his breath. So far, so good.

The pain roared its fiery breath at him, but he was determined to walk. Standing upright was already a victory. The strategy of resting and waiting it out, had failed. *Fuck the pain!* He thought. He let go of the chair and stood on his own. Once he had his balance, he slid one foot forward and then the other. In short fits and starts, he made it to the door. Stepping outside, he felt infinitesimally small before the enormous backdrop of blue sky, a point of pain in unlimited space. The one-inch steps posed a terrifying challenge. There was no railing to hold onto. Standing at the top, he felt like an Olympic ski jumper about to thrust himself down the mountain. He wasn't sure how to do it. It was almost impossible to stand on two feet. How could he rest on one? He bent his left leg ever so slightly and came down a step on his right. Success. Thank God for small risers!

The pain had changed from purple to red to black as he slowly inched his way forward. He was making progress, though. He passed by Tuffy and started down the path to Meera's cabin. She would be startled to see him. He wondered how he'd make it back up, but he'd figure that out later. As he continued, though, his mood darkened. He felt utterly compromised, practically defeated. *I can't continue to live like this,* he thought. He tried to deconstruct what was happening in his mind and body, concentrating on the difference between the actual physical pain he felt and the fear of pain, which he was convinced was the cause of the vice-like spasms that wrapped him in a strait jacket. Fear is the mind-killer, he reminded himself. The more he focused on this distinction between the fear and the pain, the more acutely he saw their differences and their relationship. *OK, God,* he said to himself, *I can take the pain, but I'm no longer willing to accept the fear.*

He stopped his pathetic shuffling, turned around and made a decision to run up the hill, no matter what the consequences. *I'd rather break my back and go to the hospital, if that happens, than live like this anymore,* he told himself. He gritted his teeth, and with a burst of maniacal will power, sprinted up the path. He ran madly up the hill, ecstatic. He couldn't believe it. The pain was still there, red hot and angry, but the strait jacket had disappeared. He stopped by his wood pile, picked up the 15-pound split mall and started madly chopping wood. Deliriously happy, he realized with a sense of awe that this was the epochal moment of his life.

Sasha could not wait to share this with Jeffrey. Jeffrey above all would understand. Bursting with optimism and energy, he put down his maul and headed towards the path to Jeffrey's house. It seemed like a million birds were chirping, singing halleluiahs to him. He practically danced down the path. When he arrived, he knocked briskly on the door and opened it, not waiting as he usually did. What he saw stopped him in his tracks. Meera was on the floor with her arms around Jeffrey's legs, her head in his lap. For a moment, he thought Jeffrey was sleeping. But when Meera turned her head, he could see that she was crying and Jeffrey was gone. He went over to her and held her, sobbing in his arms. Somehow, he knew, Jeffrey was responsible for his epiphany.

Chapter 24

So, how goes it, Lar? I've been missing you. I hope you will take seriously my invitation to visit. You and Marsha would think this was heaven. It's turned very hot. Spring passed by like an afterthought. My garden is a real garden now. I have beans and peas growing up elaborate trellises I built from madrone branches and tomatoes that threaten to outgrow their cages, rows of corn and mounds of squash and zillions of onions, eggplants and a deliriously delicious patch of strawberries that I inherited. I have not thought of a single Russian revolutionary since I arrived. My pot plants are looking sturdy and are badly wanting to be put in the ground. Meera's going to help me sex them tomorrow.

She and I have grown close, but neither of us seem ready to take it any further. We probably eat together three or four times a week and have taken to reading books out loud to one another. She's taught me how to make my own tofu and yogurt and various breads. We tend to buy things in bulk, like fifty-pound bags of brown rice, because going into town to shop is an all day venture. We've begun to get a few things out of our gardens. Soon, though, we'll be overcome with vegetables. I don't know what we're going to do with this bounty. Meera is a master gardener. Marsha will love her.

I've also heard from Darlene. Sounds like she's definitely going to visit at harvest time. I'm still not sure whether she's coming alone (In Shallah) or with her beloved Rolfie (God forbid). I dream about her a lot, probably too much.

My friend and neighbor Jeffrey died. It was a very big loss for me. I had never had a mentor before and I can only guess now how much more I might have learned from him, had he lived longer. But he was old. I think 93 or 94. He had an amazing life and a good death. Bruce and Kimmy drove his body to nearby Fortuna for cremation. We're planning a celebration here in a few days to scatter his ashes by the creek below us. It's quite a hike to the creek, but in this heat it's well worth the trek. You can fully submerge and get wet, but it's not deep or big enough to really swim. It's extremely beautiful though, lots of clear water rushing over large boulders cut off from the rest of the world. I go down there probably every other day. Yesterday, Meera and I went down and almost walked right into a family of bears bathing. This big thing came out of the water right in front of me. At first, I thought it was a dog, but what I saw was just its head. The rest of its body followed. She probably weighed 600 pounds or more, I'd guess. When she saw us, she turned and walked out of the creek on the other side, luckily for us. She shook off the water like a dog. Then two baby bears emerged and followed the momma bear. Life on Grizzly Mountain!

Dobbyn Creek is a huge relief from the heat. It was a hundred today. But by the time you walk all the way back up the half mile trail, you're ready for another dip. Carl built a small pond next to the yurt, but it's useless, filled with weeds and I don't like swimming in it. To really swim, we go to the Alderpoint beach, an idyllic setting with clean white sand dunes and large rock formations in the middle of the river that look like those paintings you often see of China. We will definitely spend a lot of time there when you and Marsha come. Right now, we're too busy with the pot and the gardens to go more often; but once everything gets in the ground, we'll probably go almost every day.

A bunch of my friends up here got together and bought the land around the swimming hole and created a conservancy to keep it from ever being developed. Everyone goes naked there. It's quite a scene. Hopefully, Marsha will be able to keep you from gawking at the girls. There's a surprising number of beautiful young women, actually, but none of them stay single for very long. Meera's the only exception that I know. There seem to be a few single guys, but all the girls are taken. I had a dream about a girl in clown white that was so vivid I almost drove seven hours to San Francisco to find her. I'd love to share this paradise with a lover, but I am learning to live on my own for now. That's the big lesson for me up here. Part of the challenge is purely logistical, learning how to fix your car when it breaks down, or repair the water line or fix the road. But the bigger challenge is learning how to live with yourself.

One of the biggest differences is how much time you have to think. There aren't the normal distractions that occupy one's time in society. I'm not on the phone or talking with people all day, or planning what to do. There just are the everyday acts of living—picking up twigs and branches for kindling, weeding the garden, feeding the dog, tending the pot and, oh yes, I almost forgot, gathering eggs! I've become the proud father of three beautiful girls—a Rhode Island Red, a Barred Plymouth Rock and an Araucana, whose eggs are blue and green like Easter eggs. They give me fresh eggs every day, though they like to play hide and seek with them. I had to build them a chicken coop to protect them at night, but they roam free all-day long. They each have names. Georgia, the Araucana, lets me hold her. The others are kind of skittish. She once laid an egg in my hand as I held her! A hot egg! I was very touched. I got them when they were already old enough to start laying.

Bruce helped me build the coop. It was the first thing I'd ever built in my life. It sits off the ground on pier blocks, with four by eight plywood sides and a roof covered in a roll of tar paper. It has a little ramp up to a door. Inside the floors are covered with straw or old newspapers, if I'm out of straw, which I have to shovel when the smell is too bad. They've each got their own little boxes to nest in and a dowel across the length of it for roosting. I lock them in there each night and let them out in the morning after I get my fire going and before tai chi. I've left an egg marked with an X in each of their boxes, so they're never without an egg under them. It's amazing how many eggs they produce. If I don't check for a while, I'll come out with a whole basket full. Lately, though, they've been hiding their eggs in the grass and woods around the house. Georgia likes to lay her eggs in a pile of kindling I keep on the deck in a large wicker basket. I think she wants to move in with me. They are so funny. I can watch them for hours. You can see almost every human trait in them—greed, vanity, jealousy, everything. Watching them is as entertaining as watching reruns of *I Love Lucy*. Best of all are the eggs. There's nothing quite like eating fresh eggs. I have them almost every day.

Well, that's it for today. Please write and tell me about life in the real world. Are you happy and healthy or just horny? Do you ever run into Sarah or hear about her and Alice? Tell me everything. I think about you and Marsha coming here a lot. It will be so great to show you this life.

Your very own Sasha.

Chapter 25

The post office had the only air conditioning in town. It was already 100 when Sasha pulled up to the square brick building with an American flag outside, a building that looked wholly out of place among the ramshackle cottages of Alderpoint. "Hi Marge," he said.

"Hey, Sasha." Marge's greeting conferred his status as a genuine local. "I've got a letter for you, just arrived." She went in the back and came out with a bundle of junk mail and letters. "Can you take these up to Bruce, Kimmy and Meera? I was sorry to hear about the old man. I liked Jeffrey. He always kidded me, made me laugh. I'll miss him."

"Yes, won't we all." He recognized his mother's handwriting and decided to wait until he got back home to open it. He put the mail on the front seat of his truck and told Caliber to wait in the back. "I'll be right back." Walking down the road to the store, he heard a chain saw chewing a log down by Chief Redman's house on the way to the river. He recognized the two guys sitting on hickory chairs on the store's porch passing a joint and nodded hello. The screen door screeched.

There were flies buzzing about. It smelled of fertilizer: bags of cow manure, blood meal and bone meal were stacked high against the walls. Most people bought their pot supplies in Garberville, but if you lacked anything, you usually could find it here for twice the price. Going over the hill to Garberville was an all-day affair, so it sometimes was worth it. Sasha walked to the back and picked up a gallon of milk and some cheddar cheese from the fridge, grabbed a bag of chips, thought twice about it before putting it back, and bought a chocolate covered Häagen-Dazs ice-cream bar for the ride home.

When he was alone again in Tuffy, he glanced at the letter on the seat next to him. Letters from his parents inevitably brought up some bad feelings. They were careful never to second-guess his decisions, which he appreciated, but he knew how alarmed they were that he had left the university. He didn't tell them how he would support himself, but he assumed they could guess. His truck roared to life with a comforting confidence. Tuffy was getting pretty loud, though, Sasha thought to himself. He'd look into getting him a muffler when he was next in Garberville. He pulled out of the small town and onto the county road, turned on the bridge over the Eel and drove on the paved road along Dobbyn Creek. On his right, fields of tall blond grass swayed with the wind. These gentle bald hills were cow country, cowboy country. The annual rodeo was this month in Fortuna. He wondered what those ranchers must think about the wave of hippies coming to Southern Humboldt.

As he turned up his road, he scared a pack of buzzards which were feasting on carrion. Then he saw, for just a moment, a shape run back towards the woods. It took him a second to register that it was a bobcat, only the second one he had seen since he arrived on Grizzly Mountain.

When Tuffy pulled up to the yurt and Sasha turned off its engine, the sound of silence spread over the hills. He savored this moment as the echo slowly disappeared from his ears. Jumping out, he opened the hood and attached the cables that ran from the house to his battery. Just driving to town and back would recharge the battery enough for a couple weeks' worth of power for his reading lights and music. He took his groceries and the mail into the yurt and sat down at the table to read the letter from his mother.

His grandmother had passed, she told him. He suddenly felt very alone. Grammy was his favorite. She had been sick for a long time, so it was no surprise. Grammy was warm and affectionate, the opposite of his mother. He thought of all the times Grammy comforted him, of the day she made him chocolate pudding after he scraped himself falling from his bike, the week he spent on the sofa at her apartment when he had the mumps. He loved sitting on her large lap snuggled up against her ample bosom while she turned the pages of the family albums she kept. His grandfather had been long gone, a kibbitzer who shot at flies on the ceiling with a BB gun. Grammy's death was the passing of a generation. He never knew his grandparents on his father's side.

Alone in the yurt, he didn't know what to do to express his grief. He had had very little practice. Instinctively, he led Caliber outside and walked up the path along the pond towards the water tank. Halfway to it, Caliber stopped at the sudden sound of a rattle. Sasha coaxed him back to his side and circled wide around the snake. "Good dog, good dog," he said petting him. People thought of rattle snakes as bad, Sasha reflected, but he was intrigued by a survival mechanism that relied more on warnings than on venom. *If only humans had evolved like that*, he thought. Off the path now, he veered straight up the hill to a lone willow tree that stood by itself on a slope of golden grass. It was cool under its canopy. He sat down and slowly cried. His thoughts went from his grandmother to Jeffrey. He hadn't cried yet for him. *This will be my grief tree*, he told himself. Looking out over the rolling hills below him, at the shimmering sky, Sasha felt himself at peace.

He didn't know how long he sat like that. He had started to meditate, a practice that he had begun to do every day, but soon fell into a trance or sleep. When Caliber woke him, Sasha didn't immediately open his eyes. When he did, Meera was standing in front of him. Neither of them said anything. Finally, he asked, "How long have you been here?"

"Not long, just a couple of minutes. You looked so peaceful," she said. "I didn't want to disturb you."

"My grandmother died. I was just sitting here thinking about her."

"I'm sorry," she said. "You never spoke about her. Were you close?"

"Yes, quite, though I haven't seen her in two or three years. She was the one I could always count on, no matter what trouble I was in. I was her only grandchild, so she doted on me."

She gave him a hand. He stood awkwardly. Then, she stepped towards him and put her arms around him. When he stepped back, he smiled. "Thanks. That felt good."

"I stopped by to see if you wanted my help sexing your plants. They should be ready now."

"I'd love that," he said. He pointed to the spot where the rattle snake was. "Be careful, there's a rattler there near the path."

"Thanks. They love to sun themselves on the open dirt."

As they walked down the hill towards the path, Sasha silently said his goodbyes to his grandmother. She would like Meera, he thought. Meera was kind and comforting, like she was.

Meera walked ahead of him around the back of the yurt, under the dappled light of the madrone trees, and through the garden gate. The sun was directly overhead. The days had become predictably hot with clear skies and little, if any, humidity. It would stay like that through the rest of the growing season, Meera assured him. Her skin had already browned, accentuating her Middle Eastern features. She was wearing a blue print Balinese sarong, crossed and tied at her neck, a straw hat with an extra-wide brim, large plastic sunglasses and a pair of leather sandals. Sasha had on the same pair of frayed khaki shorts he wore everyday with no shirt, no sunglasses and no shoes. He no longer had to watch where he walked. His body had become thin and muscular.

Watching Meera from behind, he could fully take in her body and he felt himself aroused. He imagined himself stopping her and pulling her down on the ground in a moment of passion. But what if she rejected him? She hadn't given him any reason to believe she was attracted to him. It would be a devastating blunder that would disrupt the delicate balance of living together on Grizzly Mountain. It could ruin their relationship and leave him desperately alone. He couldn't risk it. The stakes were too high and, besides, she was still married to a phantom that was, apparently, all too alive.

At the entrance to the garden sat the plants in a long row against the fence. All 102 of them survived the transplanting. Sasha was proud of them. They had branched out and grown to about three-feet tall, touching their neighbors. Vibrant and healthy, they seemed to call out to be put in the ground and freed to grow big and strong. Meera bent down to examine them. "They look great, Sash," she said.

"Thanks to your help transplanting them," he answered.

She looked up and smiled. "Notice how some of the stalks are beefier and have subtle purple veins running down them. I bet those are from the triple cross seeds Charles gave you." They lifted the planter up and saw three X's on some masking tape. "The plants that are a little taller and a little sparser are more likely males, but we need to check the nodes for balls," she said.

Sasha laughed. "Of course." He bent down next to her. She smelled sweet like hibiscus.

She gently lifted one of the branches up and pointed to the node where the branch attached to the stem. "See those two tiny sacs nestled in there? Those are the balls. The females look very much like that, so distinguishing them can be tricky. The girls have little stigmas, little translucent hairs that grow from the tops of their sacs, which are slightly more elongated than the males. Here," she took another plant and spread its branches to show him. "These sacs are a little more slender. Can you see the two tiny hairs growing off them? They're your girls."

Sasha closely examined several of the plants. "This is what it must feel like to be a gynecologist," he joked. "I'm a little embarrassed."

"You'll have your very own harem soon, but we've got to exile these nasty boys far enough away that your girls will remain virgins. It's kind of cruel, actually. But you'll have your chance to impregnate some selected branches to breed next year's seeds. That's my favorite part in this process. It's very intimate. We get to be directly involved in the mating process and then become midwives. It never stops amazing me," she said. He wanted to say something, but kept it to himself.

"It is amazing to be so intimately involved in another species' reproductive life," he said. "We become the selector in their natural selection. It makes a lot of sense though, doesn't it? These females produce flowers that literally turn us on too, just like they attract the male pollen. That's their survival advantage."

"We'll determine which ones are the males now and move them far enough away that the wind won't carry any of their pollen here," Meera explained. "One male plant could deflower your whole garden and ruin your crop. No one anymore wants to buy pot that has seeds in it. The virgin girls are ten times more powerful than ones who've put all their energy into producing seeds. It does feel a little unsisterly of me to deny them this pleasure, but it's all in the cause of an ever-stronger species." She made eye contact with Sasha. "You'll have to keep looking out for these male sacs throughout the growing season. Some of the plants can turn hermaphrodite up until harvest. The worst thing that can happen to your crop is for your plants to be fertilized by a hermaphrodite. They'd make seeds and, worse, the seeds would tend to be hermaphrodite too. But if you pay attention, you won't have a problem."

They spent the next hour culling the male plants and carried them, six pots at a time, to a small clearing down past the outhouse about a hundred yards below the garden. They would stay in pots until their pollen was harvested. Sasha told the boys not to feel bad. He'd collect some of their pollen for the best girls, he promised them. When they finished they counted the females that remained, 54 of them. "I only have space for 25 in the garden," said Sasha. "But I've been thinking of digging holes below the yurt and running all my grey water to them."

"Great idea," she said. "Why not? The grey water will have its own nutrients. They'll like that. But you won't be able to wash with soap or detergent. In any case, you're out in the open growing in the garden, so you might as well do them all. It'll be a good size crop."

He stepped towards her and put his arms around her. "Thanks, Meera. I wouldn't know what to do without you."

Chapter 26

Summer ruled with sovereign persistence. Days became indistinguishable from one another, the sun glaringly hot in a relentlessly blue sky, the tempo of all things living slowed to a crawl. The heat imposed its order on the land: work in the garden in the early morning, weeding and watering, cleaning out the chicken coop, gathering eggs. The pot plants were now as tall as Sasha. He had managed to plant twenty-five more holes below his yurt, irrigated with an elaborate system of PVC hoses and drip lines. It took all morning to water these and the upper garden, and the few male plants he kept for breeding. He picked yellow shade leaves off the females to let in more light. It was all a meditation. By lunch time it would be too hot to do much more.

Each afternoon he would drive to town, usually with Meera, sometimes with Bruce and Kimmy, and park along the railroad tracks above the Alderpoint beach. The trail down to the beach cut a canyon through walls of blackberries. They would pick and eat their way down and then cross the hot white sand dunes to the emerald green Eel River. Nirvana.

There was no shade unless they brought their own umbrella. The dogs liked to stay close, but the sand burned their paws and they retreated up the dunes to a line of trees and small shrubs. There were usually a dozen or more people, all naked, all growers. Sasha was one of the only men without a beard. Everyone was tan and slim. They shared their food from their abundant gardens. Joints passed continuously.

But today would be a break from his routine. He had discovered an envelope Carl had left him which he had stashed away among his piles of books and then forgotten. It was a gift of LSD, which Carl vouched for, having tripped on it many times with Kimmy. Meera had agreed to take it with him. He naturally had some fear dropping acid for the first time, but he'd be with Meera. What better guide could he ask for?

He finished watering his gardens and was sitting on his deck checking Caliber for ticks. He pulled off a dozen of them, separating their heads from their bodies. A few had bored in. Sasha pulled them out carefully, trying to avoid leaving the head in. Sometimes he had to put a burnt match to the tick to get them to let go. It was easy to find them on Caliber's blond fur and the dog loved it when Sasha fussed with him. Meera and Lady Jessica came up and the Lady stood obediently still as Sasha searched her as well, mostly feeling for them through her dark coat. She was clean.

"I hate these things," said Sasha.

"Me too," said Meera. "I check myself and Lady Jessica several times a day." She looked up and around her. "It's a beautiful day for tripping. Not too hot yet. I thought we might walk in the woods for the shade. Later, we can go down to the creek and get wet, if we want."

"Sounds great to me," said Sasha. "Should we take it on any empty stomach?"

"Sure," said Meera.

"Have you had any of this batch before?" asked Sasha.

"Probably. I've tripped quite a few times with Kimmy and Carl. Let me see it." He handed her the envelope and she took out a small strip of blotter acid on paper with tiny drawings of Mickey Mouse on a grid. "Oh, it's Mickey. I know Mickey. He and I are friends. Mickey, meet Sasha."

He pulled up a pair of scissors from his Swiss Army knife and cut out two of the little squares. "Hard to believe that something this small can do what it does," he said, passing one of the pea-sized pieces to Meera's outstretched hand.

She didn't hesitate putting it in her mouth. They stared at each other for a moment, then laughed. Then Sasha followed suit.

"How strong is it?" Sasha asked.

"You won't have any trouble. It's the real deal, but we're only taking two hundred micrograms. You'll be fine. But you won't be the same after that," she warned.

"That's exactly what I want. I need to stretch."

"Let's get out of here while we're still straight and it's not too hot," said Meera. "I want to take you on an old Indian trail through the woods that Charles showed me. It's beautiful and we can't get lost. It's on the way down to the creek.

Bring some water."

184

They headed downhill towards Little Dobbyn Creek, then veered across a rocky ridge and entered the woods through a grove of oaks and madrone that soon gave way to tall virgin fir trees. The dogs led the way, excited to be on such an adventure. The path was surprisingly worn, probably from deer. They walked in silence. A slight breeze rustled the leaves in a hush.

About twenty minutes after dropping the acid Sasha began to be fixated on the sound of the forest floor under his bare feet. His stomach began to feel like he was on a ship. He slowed his walk, then stopped and turned to Meera. "I think I feel something," he said. Meera's face had become a collage of colors: cheeks flushed pink like cotton candy, eyes the color of green bottle glass, her hair menacingly alive and, as Meera opened her mouth to speak, Sasha realized she looked like Mrs. Milligan, his friend Arthur's mother whom he had a mad childhood crush on.

"Me, too," Meera spoke, but it sounded like her voice came from a tunnel. They both started laughing and the more they laughed, the faster the acid seemed to come on. Tears ran down their cheeks. Every time they came close to stopping, they'd start up again. When their laughter finally subsided, Sasha looked around at the woods and down below at the creek rushing across boulders and rocks and felt a wave of euphoria and well-being. How could he have not seen all the life that was pulsing around him before, he wondered. Everything was super vibrant and whenever he stopped to look carefully at anything, a leaf or a piece of bark, he realized with awe that it was moving, undulating like molecules seen under a microscope.

185

He lifted his arm and it, too, was a moving, changing, swelling piece of flesh. He could almost see the blood coursing through his veins.

He tried to tell Meera that she looked like Mrs. Milligan, but every time he got to the name, he started laughing again. Miriam was in her own world, a look of wonder, like a child's, on her ruddy face. There were birds chirping overhead and they seemed to be communicating directly with them. In fact, everything seemed to all be part of some living, breathing whole. As he thought this, Sasha felt a breeze blow through the forest, saw the leaves dancing to it as if a conductor were choreographing their movements and then, to his astonishment, realized that his own breath was part of this ensemble. He breathed in and savored the rich earthy aromas of the woods and when he breathed out it was part of the wind that danced all around him. It was as if the forest were breathing him.

It was at that moment that Sasha had a spiritual epiphany. He was experiencing reality directly, as a new-born infant might. All of our conceptions, all of our descriptions, indeed, language itself were limiting, modifying and reducing this reality to ideas in our heads, exactly as Jeffrey had told him. He had spent a lifetime mistaking these mental images for reality itself, but that was a lie, a veritable misperception. How easy it was to look beyond that screen and see what was around him. Nature was practically shouting at him to watch and listen, to get out of his head. He felt as if some physical straps that had encased him in an artificial reality had suddenly come loose. He was free now, like that squirrel over there, to be part of the real nature. All the previous measures of life—job titles, academic degrees, fame, money, status, all of it, seemed ridiculous, pathetic. He began to run, ecstatic with the strength of his naked feet, oblivious to the minor pains, enjoying them for the truth they told. He had done it. He had transformed himself from tenderfoot to Indian warrior. He let out a wild yelp of triumph that echoed through the forest.

Then he stopped and stood perfectly still in heightened awareness of his surroundings. Colors were more vivid, sounds more distinct, lights brighter. He closed his eyes and felt like he still knew exactly where every leaf and twig were. When he opened them, he began to recognize the patterns of nature around him and it was then he had his second revelation. It struck him as a huge metaphysical truth about the world. Every life form had its own pattern and there was a pattern of patterns, a mosaic of life, in which every living thing interacted, and were connected, as parts of a single whole. And these patterns constituted a kind of intelligence. That's how they proliferated. He picked up an acorn from the ground and realized with a sense of reverence that the acorn contained a design that would best adapt it to its environment, grow and reproduce. What could constitute greater intelligence than that? It was, in fact, what intelligence was all about. Against the entropy of the universe, there was a holy creation. *God*, he said to himself with reverence, *was nothing more than intelligence.*

He was overcome, in utter wonderment, in worship. When Meera finally came upon him sitting along the path, Sasha wanted to explain what he had understood, but heard himself say, instead, "Meera, you're the most beautiful woman in the world." He stood. She was standing close to him, almost his height. He could feel her breath on his face. He could see the whole universe through her eyes. His hands moved to her waist. But before he moved to kiss her, she stepped back and began to laugh and, suddenly, they were both on the ground laughing convulsively, unable to stop. When they finally did and could catch their breath, they walked back along the path holding hands. When they reached Meera's cabin, to his amazement, he learned that almost five hours had passed.

Chapter 27

Sasha woke in the predawn stillness before the night broke to the sounds of birds. He pictured them sleeping, snuggled in their downy softness and wondered what they dreamt about. It was an important day, he reminded himself. Larry and Marsha were coming, along with their eight-year old daughter Natalie. He could not remember being so excited about a visit before. Ever since he had arrived on Grizzly Mountain he had imagined sharing with Larry the show and tell of his daily experiences. Soon he would share them in real time. They were taking the early morning bus up from Oakland and would be arriving in Garberville around 1.

He started a fire in the cook stove for coffee. He was almost out of kindling. There would be so much to do to get ready. He had bought two air mattresses and borrowed pillows and enough bedding from Meera and Kimmy. Food he'd get in town before the bus got there, if he made it in time. The biggest problem and the greatest crisis he had faced since his arrival was a plague of grasshoppers that threatened to devour his entire crop. For the last seventy-two hours he had battled them to exhaustion, picking off thousands of them, one every couple seconds, separating their heads from their bodies until his arms turned red with blood. It was gruesome. He was the "Adolph Eichmann" of the insect world, he told himself. The image of a grasshopper face haunted him as he tried to sleep. He would do all he could to protect his crop before leaving for town, but he feared there might be little left when he got back.

It's probably time to break down and get a 12-volt hot water maker, he told himself, waiting impatiently for the water to boil. He had resisted buying any time-saving devices which, he knew, was a slippery slope back to the life of convenience he was escaping. He had given a lot of thought to this, had even started taking notes for writing a critique of modern life, which he believed could be explained by our insatiable need for speed and the seduction of conveniences. It will only get worse, he knew. Wars are won by advantages of speed. Highways, computers, nuclear chain reactions, they were all part of humanity's inevitable acceleration to what? The coffee water finally came to a boil and he forced his mind back to the tasks at hand. The yurt needed to be swept, the lanterns cleaned and their wicks cut, the beds inflated and made up. He'd bring in a zillion flowers from his garden.

By the time day broke on the horizon and a chorus of song birds welcomed the first rays of sun, he had already finished his breakfast and prepared the house for his visitors. He came back from the garden with an armful of flowers, which he placed in every conceivable vessel, even filling the sink with pink phlox and yellow snapdragons. He would skip tai chi and meditation this morning. He fed Caliber, let the chickens out of their coop and started watering his gardens. The pot plants were well over his head now. He had Meera take a Polaroid with his arms outstretched under a towering cannabis tree and mailed it to Darlene. She was coming, she wrote back, just before harvest and her trimming gig in Honeydew. There was no mention of Rolf this time. Sasha prayed she would come alone.

As he left to drive over the hill, the sun had gripped the Earth in a straight-jacket of heat, shimmering off the asphalt as he turned from the dirt road onto the county road. A cloudless blue sky and the absence of any breeze offered no hope for relief. A fox turned to look at him, its head drooping. A gaggle of geese headed up river honking. There would just be enough time to get to Garberville before their bus. They could help with shopping, he thought, probably better that way. He was very excited. He couldn't wait to show them his scene and his new life.

He drove into Garberville just as the Greyhound bus pulled up to the convenience store on the main drag, releasing its air brakes with annoying scorn. The doors opened. A few scraggly locals carrying boxes and bundles, a young hippie chick smelling of patchouli oil with a blonde braid that hung past her butt, and an old man with a staff looking like Father Time disgorged from the front of the bus. A good minute passed causing Sasha some anxiety before Natalie jumped from the bus and, blinking in the bright sunlight, recognized Sasha and ran to him like a lost friend. Larry and Sasha hugged each other. Marsha, looking down at his shoeless feet, said, "Well,

Professor Simonov, you do look the part," then stepped forward and wrapped her arms around him.

"Hot enough for you?" asked Sasha. "How was your trip?" He took them to the Eel River Café for lunch. Natalie scrutinized the various characters seated at the counter with amazement. Sasha told them the problems he was having with a "biblical plague" of grasshoppers. Marsha couldn't wait to see his garden. When Natalie ventured to the bathroom they whispered to Sasha that she knew nothing about marijuana and they hoped to keep it that way. "I'll tell her the tall plants in the garden she sees are pineapple trees," Sasha said. After they ate, they walked back to the truck and met Caliber who covered Natalie's face with wet kisses. Sasha poured some water for him into a bowl. Then they went shopping for food. Natalie insisted on riding in the back with Caliber when they drove back over the hill and after a heated argument, they agreed when Sasha assured them that all the kids around there did that.

The ride to Alderpoint worked its magic on them. They ascended higher and higher through bald hills blanketed with golden grasses, yellow Scotch broom and purple lupine to ever greater vistas of openness and a vast empty silence. There were no fences, only the occasional cattle guard rattling under them in the road and in the distance stood Jarrett Peak above the endless horizon. Marsha kept turning to check on Natalie whose wind-swept face had a look of serenity she had rarely seen before. They passed by several deer. Caliber went back and forth from side to side biting at the wind.

When they reached Alderpoint, Sasha drove down and parked by the railroad track. "This will be a real treat for Natalie and for you," he said. "Bring sunscreen, if you have it. I've got blankets and a shade umbrella." They packed chips and cold drinks and headed down the narrow path through a cornucopia of blackberries, then down sand dunes to the river's edge. "We come here pretty much every day," Sasha told them. There were already several groups of naked young men and women scattered about and the smell of pot wafted from them, but Natalie seemed oblivious to it. "It's bathing suit optional," said Sasha and to his surprise Marsha and Larry disrobed without hesitation. Natalie seemed interested only in playing with Caliber, endlessly throwing stones in the water for him to chase, and in short order she, too, took off her clothes and ran into the river.

"She's like a different person here," said Larry.

"She does seem pretty content," said Sasha. "I think she and Caliber have fallen in love."

"She had a great time at camp, too, her first overnight. She came back so grown up," Marsha commented.

"That's what panics me," said Larry. "Girls can get pretty vicious in middle school. If she gets out of hand, I'll send her to her Uncle Sasha. You could use a kid."

"I've got hens. They're enough for me," said Sasha.

"You ever get lonely living by yourself?" asked Marsha.

"I do, sometimes. But I've got a good friend just down the path from me, a woman named Miriam. We all call her Meera. We've become very close. We see each other most days."

Larry lifted an eyebrow.

"No, it isn't like that, Lar. We're just friends. And you'll meet Kimmy and Bruce, too. We all help each other, but we also give each other lots of space. I like it that way."

"What do you miss?" asked Marsha.

Sasha thought about that. "Not much. Just you two, mostly. I don't miss the culture or restaurants so much, maybe newspapers and movies."

It was hard to pull Natalie away from the river. They were the last to leave. They ate their way to the truck. Marsha picked enough blackberries to make a pie. "You do have flour, don't you?" she asked.

"I do. I make my own bread. I've got everything you need."

Sasha drove them by the general store and onto the county road. The sun was getting low in the sky, but it still felt like an oven outside. He turned on Wallace Ranch Road and then onto the 3-mile dirt road that led to the yurt. Natalie could be heard singing "a hundred bottles of beer on the wall" and, just as she got down to seventy-three, Tuffy let out an explosion of steam and came to a sudden stop. Sasha jumped out and opened the hood. Steam was pouring out of the radiator. "She overheated," Sasha called to them, shaking his head. "I should have checked it before I left. Damn it!" There was no water in the truck. "We can leave everything here. Someone can give us a ride back," he said, but Larry insisted they could carry everything, if it were really only three miles; so, they gathered their suitcases and the groceries and hiked in.

They had to stop every five minutes or so to rest. They were in shade much of the way, but it was still hard to lug so much weight. Natalie was uncharacteristically cooperative, continuing to sing the whole way. By the time they rounded the last curve and caught sight of the yurt, they were drenched in sweat. Caliber barked excitedly. They dragged themselves up the one-inch risers. "Welcome to my humble home," said Sasha, opening the door to the yurt.

Inside, seated at the bowling alley table was Charles and a young derelict-looking guy in camos, also toothless, whom Sasha had never seen before. In front of them on the table was a large pile of bullets and several dismantled rifles and a pistol. A cloud of pot smoke enveloped them.

"Charles, what's up?" asked Sasha, trying to act nonchalant in the face of a small arsenal and a stranger who appeared very stoned.

"Hey, man, I came up to warn you that they busted a big grow up at Harris and one not far from here up towards Blocksburg. There were helicopters cruising Little Dobbyn. I wouldn't worry none, but thought you'd want to know." Incongruously, he had that big Charles grin on his face. "Oh, yeah, I hope you don't mind but we sampled some of the LSD you left on the table. It's sooo good," said Charles. He introduced his friend. "Sasha, this is Clancy. Clancy, this is Sasha."

Sasha managed a smile and introduced Larry, Marsha and Natalie.

"What are you doing?" Natalie asked Charles, her eyes wide.

Charles' laugh was infectious, an innocence that helped ease the tension. "We're making our own ammo," he said. "It's cheaper."

"Why do you have guns?" Natalie asked again.

"We hunt," said Charles matter-of-factly. "Ever eaten deer?"

Natalie blushed. "No," she said, suddenly shy.

"If you want, I can bring you some tomorrow. I've got some down in Bruce's refrigerator," he said. It was hard to resist Charles' good nature. He was like a child. Natalie smiled. Her fear had left her. "If you want," he continued, "I could take you to look for arrowheads tomorrow. Would you like that?" he asked.

Natalie turned to her mother for permission. "We'll see tomorrow," Marsha said, still a little apprehensive, but beginning to warm to this young man. They put down their groceries and suitcases. Charles and Clancy assembled their guns, picked up their ammo and prepared to leave.

Charles turned to Sasha. "It's so hot in here. How come you don't open the skylight?"

Sasha looked up, "Huh?" he said. "I didn't know it could open."

Charles laughed his infectious laugh. "Sure," he said "I don't know where Carl left the gizmo he had fer it, but we cut some grooves in the beams for handholds when we was building this, so's you could climb up to it, if need be," and with that he stepped on a chair and onto the table and leaped up, grabbing onto one of the beams that supported the roof, and went hand-over-hand up the beam like a kid on a monkey bar.

There was a small crank on the casement of the skylight which he turned, opening it about six inches. "You oughta clean this some time, Sasha," he said and then dropped dramatically to the floor below.

Chapter 28

"Pretty please, Uncle Sasha." Natalie begged even before it had turned light outside. "Pleeeese."

"They don't lay til I've had my coffee," he said. "I promise you'll be the one to gather them, but let me get up first." He wondered how little girls learned to be so coquettish so young. *She would not have learned it from Marsha*, he thought. "How 'bout you help me build a fire in the cookstove? Then you can get the eggs."

"They all tumbled out of their beds. A mourning dove broke the silence. "How'd everyone sleep?" asked Sasha.

"Well," they all replied.

"I dreamt I was being chased by a giant blackberry pie," said Larry.

Natalie announced, "Uncle Sasha said I could start the fire in the stove and then let the chickens out and gather their eggs. After breakfast I'm going with Charles to find Indian arrowheads."

"We'll see," said Marsha.

It was a small thing, but showing Natalie how to build a fire gave Sasha a feeling of satisfaction, of pride in all that he had learned since coming to Grizzly Mountain. The routine of living off the grid had become second nature to him. He was comfortable in this place. He had cut and chopped the wood they were using, grown the flowers that adorned the yurt and the vegetables that Marsha had begun dicing and had built the chicken coop that would yield the eggs they would eat for breakfast. He handed Natalie a basket and told her to be sure to leave one egg, the one marked with an X. "The girls don't like it, if we take all their eggs. So, I always leave them one, which I mark. If I didn't, I might leave one under them for too long." She came back in a couple minutes with six eggs.

"Is this enough?" she said. "Was that everything?" Sasha asked.

"Well, one of the hens, the red one, wouldn't let me reach under her. She kept pecking me."

"You've got to be firm," said Sasha. "She won't hurt you."

Larry took her back out and soon came in with three more eggs. Marsha had a large cast iron pan sizzling with onions and peppers, snow peas and baby squash. The smell of vegetables cooking in olive oil filled the yurt. Sasha crumbled some locally-made goat cheese. He proudly uncovered a loaf of bread he baked yesterday and warmed it in the oven.

"I'll make a pie for tonight," Marsha said.

"My friends will all stop by this evening. They want to meet you. They'd love you with a pie."

After breakfast they went on a tour of the garden. Marsha and Larry tried to keep any attention away from the pot plants, though Natalie was too busy chasing Caliber to notice anyway. When they were out of earshot, Larry said, "Holy fuck, Sasha. This is marijuana paradise! What are you feeding these beasts?" Marsha peppered Sasha with questions about his double digging techniques, his compost method, how often he watered and what he fed the plants. But their focus soon turned to the wretched grasshoppers. They watched Natalie and Caliber running through the tall grass outside the garden fence sending up clouds of grasshoppers in their wake. Even as they talked, the infestation seemed to grow. It was better having three people picking them off, but it was obvious that they probably would never get ahead of the game. Half the crop was already gone.

"Wait a second," Marsha exclaimed, exasperated. "They seem to be leaving your lower garden alone. It's cooler there in the dappled light. They like things hot and dry." She turned to Sasha. "Do you have any longer hoses?" Soon she was walking the perimeter outside the fence watering the grass, creating a wet buffer between the open grasslands and the garden and contentedly singing to herself. As Larry and Sasha continued their losing battle, picking the grasshoppers off one-by-one, they gradually could see that Marsha's plan was working. The rate of infestation was slowing. The battle would be won!

"You're a genius, general," Sasha shouted to her, "a strategic genius. Thank God you came here. I would have lost everything."

Just then Charles showed up with an old leather pouch filled with his collection of arrowheads and prehistoric stone scrappers. He poured them out on the ground. "Some of these are three or four thousand years old," he told them.

Natalie, eyes wide, examined each of them carefully. "Do you ever find beads or jewelry?" she asked.

"No, but we might. I know where we'd likely find some, if they exist. Want to come with me?"

By this time Marsha arrived. She picked up a long stone piece that came to a sharp point. "Was this a tool?" she asked.

"No. That was a spear head. See how they chipped away these bigger notches? That's how they tied it with deer guts to a wooden shaft," he explained. "They used them to hunt larger animals, even lions." He picked up a stone the size of his fist. "This here one they used to scrape the skin off their kill. I've used it, myself. Killed me a raccoon with that spear and skinned it with that there scrapper," Charles said and laughed his irresistible laugh.

"Mom," pleaded Natalie, "Can I go with Charles to look for arrowheads and beads? Pleeeese?"

Marsha looked at Sasha, who nodded his approval and held his thumb up. "OK, if Sasha thinks it safe; but be careful. You stay right by Charles and do what he tells you. Put on your sunscreen and wear your hat and bring plenty of water. It's supposed to be 105 today."

"Oh, here," said Charles. "I brought you all some deer meat. We'll make some sandwiches and take them with us."

When Charles and Natalie left, Marsha found a sprinkler to continue watering her moat and the three of them sat down under a madrone tree in the shade. Sasha lit a large joint and passed it to Marsha. She held it between thumb and forefinger like Humphrey Bogart or a European would hold a Gitane and passed it to Larry. "I didn't know you indulged," said Sasha.

"When in Rome," Marsha responded. "I love it, but I usually have too much to do to get wasted so early in the day. When Larry smokes he gets very quiet; but with me, it's the opposite. It's hard to shut me up. I jabber away and Larry listens, or pretends to. I don't like to advertise it, but I love to get high. I usually smoke when we're alone in the evening. if I lived here on a marijuana farm, I'd probably stay high all the time."

Larry seemed to be pondering something. "You know, Sash, you've been driving yourself crazy killing all these grasshoppers, but maybe you're missing a big opportunity. Grasshoppers are a great source of protein. In Oaxaca, in the markets, they sell huge amounts of them dusted with chili powder, roasted with garlic and sprinkled with lime juice. You could make a fortune, be the king of grasshoppers. We learned to eat snails from the French. Maybe we could market 'Uncle Sasha's Pot Infused Gourmet Grasshoppers,' or something."

"I feel bad for the poor things. All they're trying to do is survive and we just decapitate them," said Marsha.

Larry's face lit up, "Just imagine how stoned they must be," he said. "If we get this fucked up from a few puffs, what's it like eating your weight in fresh cannabis?" They laughed. It felt so good to Sasha to banter like this with old friends. They talked about life off the grid—Marsha thought it would be heaven and fantasized moving up here once Natalie was out of school. They weeded in the garden together in silence. The grasshoppers had clearly retreated. But it was too hot to stay out in the sun much longer, so they went back to the yurt and made lunch. As the hours passed, Marsha began to worry about Natalie. "Are you sure she's safe out there with Charles. It's so hot."

Sasha assured her that Charles wouldn't let anything happen to her, but he was also getting concerned. Sometime after lunch they heard a whistle and went out to the deck into the brutal heat and saw Charles coming up the road holding a large rattlesnake in each hand above his head with Natalie draped across his shoulder, seemingly unconscious. Marsha ran to him in a panic, but the smile on Charles' face quickly removed any fear. At the sound of Marsha's voice Natalie woke, wiggled off Charles' shoulder and ran to her. Charles held his arms high again in a victory salute. "She got a little too much sun," he said. "That's all. She'll be fine. Got us some dinner. Killed both of them with a stone, first throw." The snakes were beautiful with their mosaic skins and their delicate rattles. Each of them was taller than Natalie.

"Look Mom," said Natalie, reaching in the pocket of her shorts. She pulled out two perfect arrowheads she had found.

Larry whispered to Sasha. "She's going to have a great show and tell when we get back. 'My summer on a pot farm.'"

That evening when the sun's heat finally cooled, Meera, Bruce and Kimmy all came for dinner. There were vegetables from their gardens and Meera produced the first ripe tomatoes of the season. But the highlight was Charles' rattlesnakes. He had skinned and deboned them, then grilled them on the barbecue with some butter and soy sauce. The meat was more succulent than chicken. "Tastes like capon," said Sasha.

"What's a capon?" asked Charles.

Sasha smiled, "As my grandmother liked to say, 'A capon is a chicken that doesn't fool around.'"

Larry, Marsha and Natalie stayed for a week. They helped in the garden in the mornings and spent the heat of the day in Alderpoint at the beach, gorging on blackberries. Caliber and Natalie had become inseparable. By the time they left, it had felt like a whole summer had passed. They were brown all over. They were sad when they got into the air-conditioned bus in Garberville. Their absence left a big hole for Sasha. But Darlene should be coming soon. Now he could think of nothing except that.

Chapter 29

With Larry's family gone, Sasha's life returned to its predictable rhythm. But with the coming of harvest, a cloud of fear and paranoia began to darken the horizon of innocence and invulnerability that had reigned since he arrived. If anyone drove to the river in Alderpoint, they made sure others remained on the property to guard against thieves. The sound of a car engine or an airplane caused pulses to rise. Bruce was seen checking his various patches up the creek carrying a rifle. There were new stories of busts and rip-offs and rumors of the feds planning a massive raid. Sasha began to worry that putting his grow in the open next to his house might have been a naïve rookie's mistake.

Bruce had gone to Eureka to consult with a lawyer. The man represented most growers in the area who got busted. Bruce wanted to learn what, if anything, they could do to protect themselves. Meera and Sasha stopped by his cabin when they heard his truck pull up. Kimmy greeted them with cookies and tea. Bruce lit a joint. Sasha could feel their nervousness.

"What's the verdict?" asked Meera.

Bruce smiled. "Mark says we have little to worry about. We're too small to be on their radar. The rumors about the feds are nonsense, he said. The big danger is getting ripped off, mostly by locals, but there've been some reports of Mexican mafia moving into Humboldt. He thinks we should just stay alert. He warned me not to set any traps in the woods. He said a couple people got wounded with shrapnel from tripwire explosives some vets placed around their grows. He's representing one of them now. A couple of deer got killed that way, too. Just stay calm, he said, and don't overreact."

"What should we do, if the sheriff does bust us?" asked Kimmy.

"Run," laughed Bruce. "Probably not a good idea to leave any IDs in the house or cash. They can take that for evidence or for themselves. In fact, they can seize property like cars or land, if they bring racketeering charges. So, run, but bring any valuables with you."

"And if they do catch us?" asked Sasha.

Bruce pulled out some business cards and handed them out. Mark has your names. Just tell them to contact your attorney. I paid him a retaining fee, but he'll give it back, if we don't need anything. I think we're covered."

"It's unlikely anyone will try and rip us off in the daytime, unless it's the mafia or something," said Kimmy. "Should one of us stay up at night to listen?"

"No, that's what we've got dogs for," said Bruce. "We'll be fine. But I feel better knowing Mark can help us out, if we get in a jam."

They looked at each other and laughed. There was something surreal about this, as if it were all a game.

"The good news is that the demand for Humboldt pot is going through the roof. Some people are getting $1600 a pound in advance, I heard. If we were smart, we would hold off selling anything until the holidays," Bruce mused.

"I don't know. I just want to get our money and travel. A bird in the hand, so to speak," said Kimmy.

At that moment, Caliber started barking and all the dogs rushed outside to see what the fuss was. Everyone stayed quiet inside, listening for the sound of a motor. After a minute, Meera said, "Probably a deer." They laughed again.

"Charles told me he saw a helicopter taking bales of pot from some big bust by Harris," said Sasha. "Said it was on the evening news on KIEM. The cops apparently had a big bonfire in Fortuna. Claimed they got a ton of pot."

"Yeah, and how much did the Sheriff keep for himself?" Bruce wondered out loud.

"Well, it sounds like a lot, but they're weighing everything: stalks, leaves, roots and all," said Meera.

"That bonfire probably got the whole town stoned," said Kimmy.

The next morning Sasha woke dreaming he was in Nazi Germany, something about a cabaret and the Gestapo looking for him and Darlene singing on stage. He tried to hang on to it as he emerged into consciousness, but it evaporated. He put on his shorts and headed out to his garden, partly to reassure himself that all was well.

The cannabis plants hung heavy with buds. They had filled out, their tips now crowding their neighbors. Walking through this lush forest of pot, Sasha's arms and face became sticky with resin. The pungent odors aroused him. He rubbed his fingers together to form little beads of hash he would later dry and smoke. He pulled large yellowing fan leaves off, the ones he could reach, letting in as much sun as he could for the flowers below that were swelling in a frenzy of biological desire. Little white hairs reached out from the buds hoping to mate with the male pollen that had been denied them.

He had started early, knowing the day would soon be hot, even before his morning coffee, and now his stomach was calling for him to stop and eat. But there were endless leaves to pick and no obvious place to pause. The mindless, repetitive movement was deeply satisfying. He rarely got high in the morning, but today he started with a joint.

The ground around him was littered with yellow leaves. Nature was full of waste, he reflected. Survival came with an excess of numbers. But natural selection would soon bow to human choice. Tomorrow, with Meera's help, he would fertilize a few select branches. He was nearing the finish line in this cycle of life, a miraculous voyage from tiny seeds to plants that grew to twice his height. How could he not be in awe of this? He was a midwife in this dance of co-evolution, his mind and body turned on by the chemistry of these flowers that he would propagate to their mutual survival advantage. And turned on he was. Darlene would be arriving in two days. His dick twitched at the thought of that.

He was stark naked. The sun was now overhead. His stomach growled. The chickens were clucking on the other side of the garden fence. The air was perfectly still. He was listening to Rod Stewart in his head and picturing Darlene in Garberville, without Rolf. He didn't notice the figure approaching on horseback until it was too late to run into the yurt to put on some clothes. The man emerged on a tall horse coming directly towards him, like a slow-motion scene in a Marlboro commercial. Sasha walked through the garden gate to meet him.

The figure was mounted on a large brown stallion, a lasso hanging from its saddle. He wore a ten-gallon cowboy hat that made him look even more imposing. Sasha waited by the garden feeling totally vulnerable, naked head-to-toe and stoned, standing next to an illegal grow. As the rider approached, Sasha noticed the six-shooter in a holster by his side just above the lariat. The man towered above him on his horse. When Sasha looked up into his leathered face, he saw that it was Andy Wallace, the Chief Judge of Humboldt County Superior Court who had sold the land to Jeffrey. Someone once pointed him out when he was shopping in Arcata. For a moment, it felt to Sasha as if the end of a dream had come. He would be booted off the land, or worse. He was eyeball height to the rider's holster, when the judge leaned down and said, "Son, when those little white hairs start to turn color, at what point are they ready to pick?"

It took Sasha several seconds to comprehend what he had just heard. Although he was only inches from the man's saddle, the gulf between them was incalculable. Looking up at this rich and powerful old timer seated high above him, a cattleman whose family homesteaded this vast ranchland a hundred years before, Sasha worked to clear his mind of confusion. "It depends on what kind of high you want," he said, deciding it wasn't appropriate in this context to address him as 'your honor.' "When the white hairs, the stigma, start to curl and turn yellow and orange, you could harvest them then, but they'll get stronger and heavier the longer you wait." He was repeating what he had learned from Meera. He paused for a minute, trying to let his thoughts catch up with him. "But if you wait too long when all those hairs shrivel up and turn all-red, the pot will just put you to sleep. Something in between is usually best. How far you let them go, depends on what you like."

Judge Wallace nodded his head thoughtfully. "Mighty obliged, son," he said, turning his horse and heading back the way he had come.

Chapter 30

"Now, the magic begins," said Meera. Sasha crouched besides her, waiting. There were a dozen tall male cannabis plants, still in their plastic pots. "Pick your favorite or more than one as you wish," she said. "Half of the traits in next year's crop will come from these boys."

He examined the plants. One was a foot taller than the others. Another had a distinct purplish hue. But he was drawn to yet another, though he wasn't exactly sure why. "I like this one, but I don't know why," he said.

Meera smiled. "That would be my choice, too. Look how healthy he is. He's not the tallest plant, but he seems more compact. There's less space between nodes and," she blushed slightly, "I like how full his balls are. He looks buff."

They looked at each other and suppressed a laugh. Sasha could begin to appreciate how a pot plant might reflect the personality of the grower. Yes, this plant seemed to be the leader of the pack. Its stalk was beefy, its color vibrant. "This one does look the happiest of the lot," said Sasha. I'm pretty sure it comes from your seeds, not from Charles'."

"Yes," said Meera. "Its leaves are a little different than his." They looked under the pot and confirmed that it was.

She brought out several brown paper bags from a bakery in Arcata that were used for wrapping baguettes. "There's no wind whatsoever, a perfect day for this," she said. She pinched off a few sacs of pollen from the chosen plant and put it in one of the bread bags. "Any one of these would have enough pollen to fertilize your whole garden, so be careful. One spill could ruin your entire crop."

He picked off several more male buds and put them in the other bags. "Can we smoke these?"

"Sure. They'll give you a light high, but it's the first smoke of the year's crop and should be honored, I would think," said Meera.

They walked up the hill to the upper garden and in through the gate. "This will be harder," Sasha said. "There're so many beautiful girls. It's hard to choose."

"Man's burden," joked Meera.

But Sasha knew which plants he wanted to breed. He had his favorites. A few of them were clearly from Charles' strain with much beefier stalks that had a distinctive purple line along the length of them. They were bigger and heftier. But some of the shorter, squatter plants were more condensed and seemed to do a better job resisting grasshoppers. The stalks had short white fuzz on them. Unlike the male flowers, which hung down, the female flowers arced upwards, hoping to capture pollen from the air. Colas formed on them in clusters of conical-shaped flower buds with protruding white hairs.

There was a dominant bud at the apex. The ones with the fullest, largest and most compact buds looked like they would produce the most potent high. They were all sticky with resin. The crystals that formed along the flowers glistened in the sunlight. The sexual energy produced by so many females yearning to be pollinated was intoxicating. Sasha felt like he was surrounded by a biological orgy.

He turned to Meera. "I'm overwhelmed," he said. Smiling but silent, as if the moment were holy, Meera carefully opened one of the bags. Pollen had formed at the bottom. She dabbed a thin artist's paint brush in the pollen and handed it to Sasha, its pointed bristles coated with it. He carefully painted the flowers along a large cola at the end of one branch. At the touch of pollen, the white hairs shriveled. Startled, he almost jumped back. It reminded him of being in third grade touching a Venus Fly Trap. The intimacy of this exchange between human and plant surprised him. He was having a sexual encounter with a living plant. He could almost hear them orgasming in relief. The ones that fertilized shriveled, but the ones that didn't would just keep putting out. *No wonder pot is such an aphrodisiac*, he thought.

Meera placed the bag over the cola, sealed the bottom with twine and shook it. They looked at each other in wonder. His mind, though, suddenly flipped to Darlene and he felt a flutter of guilt. He had become very close to Meera after their acid trip and their intimacy now was awkward. He had not reminded her that Darlene would be visiting.

They repeated this process of fertilization on a half-dozen colas. When they'd finished, they retreated to the yurt for some coffee and cake Meera had brought. "That was an amazing experience," Sasha said. "I feel privileged."

Meera smiled. "I know what you mean." She paused. "You'll soon be the proud papa of hundreds of marijuana seeds that you selectively bred."

"I already feel proud," said Sasha.

They were quiet for some time. It felt to Sasha as if she had something important to say, but she remained silent. After a while she took out a joint, but Sasha raised his hand. "I'm going to be driving to town shortly, so I'll pass, if you don't mind." After a pause, he added, "I'm going to Garberville to pick up Darlene, the librarian I told you about. I mentioned it a few days ago but you've probably forgotten. She and her boyfriend are planning to trim for a friend of theirs in Honey-dew, but she's coming up here first." A pause again, "Let me know if you need anything from town."

He tried to say all this very matter-of-factly, but inside he felt positively unfaithful. Meera's face was inscrutable. She effected a smile, but he could not read beyond it. After a while she asked, "How long will she be here?" Her expression did not change.

"I don't know. A few days at least," he said. He reached for the joint nervously. "One hit won't hurt me."

They finished their coffees and Meera hurriedly got her things together to leave. Sasha didn't know what to say. He felt like he had hurt her, but there was nothing he could apologize for. She hadn't said anything, but it was what was unsaid that cut deeply. It seemed best to ignore the awkwardness. He cleaned the house and went back to the garden to pick flowers, spreading them throughout the yurt as he had for Larry's family.

He felt his heart begin to race with excitement. He was still uncertain if she were coming alone or with Rolf, but there had been no mention of him in her last letter. The dreams and fantasies he had fed since he arrived here almost a year ago were now just hours away from their realization. He tried to temper his enthusiasm which threatened to overwhelm him, but his carnal desire for Darlene, for the touch of her skin, for the taste of her mouth, for her cunt and her eyes and her hair, all of her, had lost its bridle. Oh, how desperately he wanted to make love to her!

He unplugged the cables to his battery, put down the tailgate for Caliber to jump in the back and leap into Tuffy. He felt himself propelled by an irresistible tidal wave of desire. He understood, perfectly, that there were no assurances his rendezvous with Darlene would end well. His expectations had gone through the roof, fueled by the long period of abstinence and his incessant fantasies. There was a good chance that she would be visiting with Rolf, or she could be on her period, or pregnant or, God forbid, a convert to monogamy. But Sasha would not be deterred by doubt. Like a tiger that caught the scent of his prey, he was not to be denied.

These were carbon copy days, the same unblemished blue sky, the searing heat, the stillness. There were a dozen turkey

David Hoffman

vultures circling lazily overhead as he neared the top of Alderpoint Road. He stopped for a few minutes when some stubborn cows blocked his way. He turned off his engine and listened. This was as close to heaven as one could get, he reflected. Soon, he'd be able to share this with Darlene. It was she who had changed his life and opened him to the path that led him here. Darlene who helped him overcome the repression and inhibitions that held him back and discover the truer being of his libidinal self. The memories of his times with her kept him in a fever of excitement as he descended into Garberville.

She was waiting in the shade under the awning of the Woodrose Café as he pulled up with Tuffy. Her long blonde braid hung over one shoulder and still reached almost to her waist. She was wearing a wide straw sunhat, large sunglasses, a sleeveless red blouse tied up under her breasts and a pair of short tan shorts. She saw him and waved. He jumped from his truck and walked up to her. The blood was pounding in his heart.

"You are a sight for sore eyes," he said. "You look gorgeous." He looked around. There was no sign of Rolf. "Where's Rolfie?"

"You look amazing," she said, eyeing him, coquettishly, the tip of a finger between her teeth. "Where'd you steal that body?" She looked him up and down. "You're all new."

He stepped towards her. She took off her sunglasses and looked him in the eyes. He wasn't sure how to act. He held her arms and kissed her chastely on both cheeks, stepped back and looked at her. She had the same fresh face he had dreamed about this past year, the green eyes, the freckles and the

216

dimples that opened like flowers when she smiled. There was something wholesome about her, like cut hay or mowed grass, an innocence or more like ripeness, he thought.

"Rolfie's not here," she said finally. "He took off for Honeydew. I think he may have been jealous," she giggled. "It's not at all like him. He's usually so confident."

"Maybe he could feel how turned on I am to you," he said. She looked down and didn't respond. "Have you eaten?" he asked.

They went into the Woodrose and ate enchiladas, guacamole and chips and fresh lemonade. She had a million stories about the commune, about all the hard work and the chanting and the spiritual growth they were all experiencing. She bragged about the wonderful things that Rolfie had done. Sasha told her all about his garden, the grasshoppers and Larry, Marsha and Natalie's visit. He described all the people she would meet on Grizzly Mountain. "You'll love Meera. She's the best gardener, very bright, extremely grounded and very kind." She looked up at him and held his eyes.

"Is she pretty?" she asked. He did not break eye contact.

"Quite, I suppose," he said. "She's a brunette, short hair, tall, slim graceful body."

"And she lives alone up there?" she asked. "You don't sleep with her? Aren't you attracted to her?"

He smiled. "It's not like that. We're very close, but we both guard our independence. It would be hard to have a casual sexual relationship on Grizzly Mountain. We're together every day. So, we both respect each other's space."

217

"That must get frustrating sometimes," she said. "It's hard for me to imagine you alone, without a woman, for so long."

"It is. I think about you a lot," he said.

They were quiet when they left and got in Tuffy. Caliber was asleep in the shade under the car. Sasha let him in the back. He couldn't wait to get to the beach and take off their clothes. The smell of Darlene next to him was driving him crazy. He started in first gear up the steep ascent of the Alderpoint Road when Darlene asked if she could drive. He pulled off where the road levelled out and one got the first view of the bald hills and the mountains receding to the horizon. They changed places. She adjusted the seat. She reached for the key, but then sat back, turned and stared at him. Her chest moved, her mouth parted slightly. He was delirious with desire. She moved closer. Their eyes stayed open until their mouths met and they kissed madly in utter abandon, their passions unleashed at last.

Chapter 31

On the trail down from the railroad tracks, the ground under their feet turned from stone to sand. Sasha felt like he had travelled to a parallel universe, from a world of dreams, fantasies and desires to a world of vibrant reality. This was the harvest of his months of waiting. Darlene, the goddess of his awakening, was here, incarnate, holding his hand, as they walked to the Alderpoint beach. He was drunk with the smell and feel of her.

They stopped to pick berries. It was a time of abundance. "Don't pick those low ones," he warned. "The dogs pee on them." Caliber ran ahead of them.

She turned to face him. "Open your mouth and stick out your tongue," she said, placing a ripe berry on it.

"Close your eyes and open yours," he said. When she opened her eyes, he was inches from her. He put his hands on her butt and pulled her to him. Their mouths met, tongues tasting like blackberries. Her eyes rolled back in her head. After a minute, they continued down the path, down the sand dunes to the beach holding hands.

There were still about five groups scattered on the sand. They all turned to look. He was recognized, a friend of Bruce's, a single man. Not anymore, it seemed. There was a new girl, a beautiful girl, someone that could rattle the balance of things. They all took notice.

Shade had moved across half the beach, signaling the beginning of the end of another perfect day at the river. Sasha laid out a large, colorful beach towel. Darlene kicked off her sandals, untied her red blouse, and stripped off her shorts and panties. Sasha glanced at her without staring and sucked in his breath. *Could I truly be this lucky*, he asked himself? Darlene suddenly bolted for the river. She ran like a sprinter. All eyes were on her. She was grace, power and beauty in motion. Her blond braid flew behind her like a horse's tail. Watching her from behind, Sasha felt like heaven had thrown down the gauntlet.

He rushed after her. She dove in the water ahead of him. When he caught up to her, they matched strokes heading towards a sand bar that had formed halfway across the Eel. They emerged breathing hard, bodies brown and full of glory. They held hands, walking silently along the edge of the island. Across from them most of the people still on the beach were beginning to gather towels and baskets and put on their clothes. "They'll all be gone soon," said Sasha. Darlene twirled around, dazzled by the beauty of the rocks and trees, river and sky. She came up to him and kissed him passionately. Then she pushed him back and ran provocatively to the river, challenging him to chase her. He was a lamb headed to slaughter. She could ask anything of him.

When they got back to shore, she stopped to untie her braid and immersed herself again in the river and came out shaking the sand and water from her hair like a dog. Sasha was on the towel, propped up on his elbows, lighting a joint, when she fell next to him face down, blond hair spread across her body like golden silk. They were now in the shade, but it remained warm. Two of the groups were still there, but were making moves to leave. Caliber was off by himself. Sasha lit the joint and handed it to Darlene. He lay on his side next to her. She turned to face him, inches away. He ran a finger along one of her legs, marking time, moving ever so slowly up and down and across her butt. He touched her back and brushed his fingertips over her neck and shoulders and down her arms.

Passing the joint back to him she looked into his eyes without smiling. She was still breathing hard from the swim, her breasts expanding with each inhale. From the angle they were on, he figured that his back blocked the view of the people still on the beach. He moved a finger to her breast and lightly circled her nipple. She took a sharp breath and rolled on her back. He drew his hand along the length of her legs, pausing as it brushed past the hairs between them, then around her stomach and settled on her breast. She moved his hand away. "No, not here, not now," she said, panting slightly. "They're starting to leave. Patience, my love."

The wait was agonizing. The voice of a child was an intolerable intrusion into their space. She turned on her side to face him again. They continued to look at each other. He felt like the whole universe had come to a halt. When she glanced over his shoulder, she could see the last family heading up the path with their backs to them. "Don't move," she said. She placed a finger to his lips and he kissed it, then she outlined the curves of his face, his eyes, nose and chin, then down his neck, his chest and stomach and across the top of his pubic hair and lower along his inner thigh, resting under the bottom of his balls, which hardened at her touch. His prick unfurled itself. With her thumb and forefinger, she gently stroked the length of him and rubbed the tip back and forth between them. He let out an audible gasp.

He could lay still no longer. He turned his head to see the last of the people disappearing. His hand went to her buttocks, floating around and around the soft, firm roundness of her skin. He reached tentatively up between her legs and found her opening, moist with desire. He lightly moved his finger across the lips of her cunt, teasing her. She rolled to her back and opened her legs, never letting go of his dick. His fingers spread her apart, but he held off pushing inside her. The more he waited, the greater the intensity. With a tantalizing slowness, he explored the edges of her, stroked and squeezed her clitoris. Then he slid down along her between her legs, spread apart her cunt with his thumbs and began kissing the tender insides of her, and with his fingers and mouth sucked and pulled on her clit. She gripped his head in her hands. His tongue went deep inside her. Soon, he put two fingers in her and his mouth on her clit. He felt her shutter with waves of pleasure.

She pulled him up and their mouths meshed with a passionate fury. He opened his eyes and saw hers open, fiercely staring at him. Then she rolled him on his back, slid down him and took his penis in her mouth while she stroked his shaft and his balls, faster and harder. He felt himself about to come, but held off, pulled her by the shoulders back up to him and rolled her over and entered her, plunging deep inside her. She rose up with him and, with each thrust, pressed ever closer, her hands grasping his buttocks. They rode saddled to each other with ever greater intensity until he felt the volcano of his being erupt and heard himself cry out to the ends of the world.

When he was done, she rolled him on his back, pinned his wrists on the towel and continued to hump him until she, too, came with an explosive series of orgasms that seemed to never end. Then she laid on her back next to him trying to catch her breath. Neither of them said anything. When her breathing settled, she got to her feet and pulled him up and hand-in-hand ran with him back into the river, a kind of holy baptism. When they came out, her golden hair entangled her. He came up to her and pulled it from her front exposing her breasts. He kissed them each, put his hands on her butt and pulled her close to him. Their kiss was long and sweet.

They went back to their beach towel and lay facing each other. "That's what the Gods must feel like when they make love," he said.

She smiled. "Rolf says we are most in touch with our God nature when we have sex," she said. "Sex is the gateway to enlightenment, he says."

She had told him that before. He hated hearing about Rolf. "He must be very good at it," he said, half sarcastically.

She giggled. "It's funny. He's actually quite shy. He could be with any of the other girls. He knows I wouldn't object. But he rarely has. It's not for my sake. Although he says that sex can teach us about our fears and how to get over them, I think he's actually still a bit inhibited."

Sasha couldn't help but wonder whether he could pry her from him. It bothered him how often she talked about Rolf, but he could read between the lines some seeds of dissatisfaction. They talked of life in the commune and his life growing weed and while they talked their fingers gently and absentmindedly caressed each other's genitals. After a while his penis began to grow hard again. He pushed his fingers inside her. They kissed and slowly they began making love again.

When they came to rest, Sasha said, "That was a surprise. I didn't expect that."

"I wasn't surprised," Darlene responded. "Venus just entered the fifth house."

They swam once more and watched an almost full moon come up and bathe them in light. It was twilight by the time they headed up the path with Caliber to Grizzly Mountain.

Chapter 32

In the morning, they made love again. He lay on his side snuggled against her back, indulging himself in the smell of her neck. They fell asleep like that. When he got up, he peeled the yellow strands of hair that had stuck to her skin and kissed her back. She turned to face him, purring. Her breath was stale. He got up and went outside to pee. When he returned, she was sitting up with the sheet demurely over her shoulders, her nipples showing underneath. He offered his hands and lifted her to her feet. The sheet fell away as he pulled her to him and kissed her.

"How'd you sleep?" he asked.

"I was just dreaming I was in paradise," she said, "until I realized I wasn't dreaming. Be careful, you might have trouble getting rid of me."

He smiled. "It will take quite a while to make hot water, but we can take a cold shower, if you want."

She followed him outside. The sky was thin with the morning mist, but soon to be all blue. He led her first to the chicken coop to let out the hens and gather some eggs. She walked tenderly on bare feet. They dropped off the eggs in his kitchen, gathered some towels, went back outside and turned on the shower behind the yurt. The water sputtered, then poured obediently. They held on to each other tightly. She counted backwards from twenty. He wrapped her in a blue towel and used the other to rub her limbs and her hair before he dried himself.

Inside, they started a fire in the cook stove. Sunlight now brightened the yurt. He noticed her watching him as he went through his morning rituals. This was his domain. Before, they had been in her place where she was mentor to him in his sexual and spiritual awakening. He was the neophyte being guided through her garden of pleasures. She could not help but see his transformation, in the tone of his body and the control of his environment. He was more muscular than before, particularly in his shoulders and arms, and so confident handling the hens, the stove and the cooking. He made them an omelet entirely from the vegetables he grew and the fresh eggs.

After breakfast he showed her his garden and they spent much of the morning picking pot leaves. The buds were close to ready, swollen and pungent with resin, crystals glistening in the sunlight. When they left the garden, her arms were loaded with vegetables. Watching her from behind, he felt himself stir again. Lovemaking with Darlene on Grizzly Mountain would be less a series of discrete events than a continuous dance with a few breaks for food or other necessities. Inside the yurt, she helped him hang the web of strings he'd soon use to dry the harvest.

She was standing on a chair when he ran his hands up her legs and slipped his fingers inside her shorts. She did not resist. He pulled her pants and panties down, turned her and caressed the soft flesh of her inner thighs and the wet opening of her, while she steadied herself with her hands on his shoulders. When she fell into his arms, he carried her to his mattress on the floor and they made love once again. But when he came, soon after her climax, he stifled a scream, worried that Meera might hear him. The thought disturbed him.

Spent, they fell asleep in each other's arms. It was only lunchtime when they woke up. The sour smell of sex and sweat mixed with the odor of the cannabis resin that stuck to them. There was hot water now from the stove and they went back outside and luxuriated in the shower scrubbing the pot off as best they could with a loofah. Darlene dabbed on some patchouli oil when they came inside. Sasha disliked the smell, but said nothing. "Hey, let's go down and meet my neighbors. You'll like them," he said.

They held hands on the path down to Bruce and Kimmy's hobbit cabin. The day was hot, though there were some clouds on the horizon. Bruce's dog barked as they approached. The smell of pot greeted them when they entered. Bruce, standing by the door, handed Sasha a large conically-shaped joint. "Darlene, meet my friends Bruce and Kimmy," said Sasha. "Bruce, Darlene." Bruce looked her up and down and hugged her warmly. Kimmy was standing on a chair by the sink attaching a string on one of the rafters. She smiled and nodded. Sasha thought she was not particularly friendly. Maybe they had had a fight, he wondered, or she saw any beautiful young woman as a potential threat.

"We're just hanging the first few branches," said Bruce, "celebrating the beginning of the harvest. They're a little early, but they'll still be great. I like the early buds, fresh and light. I'm real tempted to dry them quickly in the oven, but that would be a sacrilege. We'll just have to wait."

Sasha handed the joint to Darlene. "What are we smoking now?" he asked.

"This is Kimmy and Carl's fourth generation sativa. It's pretty light, good for early in the day," answered Bruce. "Have you guys eaten yet? We were just about to have some chili. There's plenty."

"Thanks. I'd love to," said Sasha, turning to see what Darlene thought.

"I'm a vegetarian," said Darlene. "Does it have meat?"

"Not a drop," laughed Bruce. "We're mostly vegetarian, too. If we eat meat, it's usually something we killed ourselves." Kimmy got down off the chair and dished some chili into bowls. They sat on the couches to eat. "So, tell us about yourself. Where you from? How'd you two meet?" Bruce asked.

Darlene answered. "At the university where Sasha taught."

"I went there, too," said Kimmy. "Were you a student?"

"Not then. I had graduated and was working in the library when we met."

"That's cool," said Kimmy. "I mostly went to the library to make out with Carl in the stacks. Never really got much into college life. We both dropped out in my sophomore year and came up here to grow. So, you graduated. What in?"

"Anthropology."

"So, what do you do with a degree like that?" asked Bruce.

"Not much," laughed Darlene. "It does help you appreciate differences between people, but that doesn't pay very well."

"I guess it qualified you to become a librarian, though."

"Well, that was just for the summer. I lived in an ashram in India for a year before I graduated. My boyfriend, who's from Germany, and I planned to move to Oregon after that to start a spiritual community."

"Did you? sked Kimmy.

"Oh, yes, we did. There are 23 of us now. We've been building houses and gardens together. It's all very communal. It's wonderful."

"And spiritual?" asked Bruce. "What do you believe in?"

"We follow the teachings of our guru, Sai Baba, but we also learn from each other. My boyfriend, Rolf, is one of Sai Baba's disciples. We believe we are all one, that God lives inside of us, not outside. Our true nature is pure love. We just need to get rid of our fears and inhibitions that keep us from that and love everyone around us."

"What if they're assholes or Hitler?" he asked dismissively.

"Rolf says they're the ones who need our love the most."

"Too bad Jeffrey's not here," said Bruce. He lived in the house just behind this, but he died a couple months ago. He wrote books about enlightenment and Eastern philosophy. He would have loved meeting you," said Bruce. He thought for a moment, then asked, "Is your boyfriend, the disciple, enlightened?"

Darlene laughed. "Oh, yes, well, most of the time. He teaches us how to be like children again. I've never seen him be judgmental."

"What's he think of your being up here with the Professor?" asked Bruce. Kimmy looked back and forth between Sasha and Darlene.

Darlene laughed. "He won't admit he's jealous, but I know he is." She turned and looked at Sasha and said, "He should be." Sasha blushed. Then she asked, "What are you going to do with this guy Jeffrey's house, now that he died?"

Bruce replied, "I don't know. We've never discussed that. I guess some lucky guy, or girl, will find her path to it. It's a simple place, but it will do. Would you like to see it?"

When they finished eating, they walked to Jeffrey's place. It was strange being there without him. Darlene looked at everything carefully, even ran the water. "Who owns this now?" she asked.

"Legally, it's Meera. You haven't met her yet, have you?" asked Bruce.

Sasha looked on with amusement, but was surprised by a certain hesitancy he felt. He had imagined wooing Darlene from her beloved Rolf, but had always pictured her in the yurt with him. What if she were to move into Jeffrey's house? Was he, in reality, ready to join his life to hers? The image in his mind of two women living alone on the property confronted him with a choice he had suppressed. His longing for Darlene was profound, but could it become love? Could he imagine living with her for the rest of his life? And what about Miriam?

"No," Darlene answered Bruce. "I haven't, but I've heard a lot about her."

Kimmy watched with some trepidation, as Darlene continued looking around the house like a prospective buyer. "Have you ever lived in the woods by yourself?" she asked.

Chapter 33

When they walked back up the path to the yurt, the clouds that had begun to form on the horizon had grown and a fresh breeze carried the first hints of Fall. There was the slightest smell of leaves in the air. Caliber sprinted ahead of them. The rains would be coming soon, Sasha thought. He was anxious to bring in the harvest before they did. Darlene reached for Sasha's hand. She walked with a gait that was long and high, as if the ground under her had springs. He could see how happy she was. He worked to keep up with her. When they got to the road, she turned and threw her arms around him and kissed him passionately.

She took the steps to the yurt in two strides. As soon as they entered, she threw off her blouse and untied the rope that held up Sasha's pants. She was not to be denied. She led him to the mattress and pushed him on his back and pulled off her shorts. Her breasts swayed over him as she mounted, her hands pressed against his chest. The whites of her eyes showed, her mouth was open and her head tossed back. She came in small ripples that built into a crescendo that crested with a roar of excruciating pleasure. Sasha was sure they could hear her in the cabins below. He worried what Meera would think.

Panting, she rolled off him onto her back. He had not come, but his dick softened and went limp. He thought about turning and kissing her, but remained where he was. His mind stayed on Meera. What would she think of this love Goddess who had invaded his home? He hoped she hadn't actually heard them. Had he made some mistake bringing Darlene into their paradise? She turned to look at him.

"What are you thinking about Sash? You seem distracted," she said.

"I was just wondering how it would be if you lived here," he said.

"Why, are you afraid I'd fuck you all the time?" she asked. "I might," she laughed. "I like it here."

They were quiet. He got up finally. "Would you like some water?" he asked, moving to the kitchen. She nodded. Their mouths were dry from the pot. He came back and handed her a glass.

"Do you regret my coming here into your space?" she asked. "You seem pretty content by yourself."

"My God, no," he said automatically. "Why do you ask that?"

"You just seemed a little distant when we made love just now," she said

"Just because I didn't come?" he said with a slight edge. "I can't come ten times a day. I'm only a man."

She laughed. "I know. I wouldn't want you to be a woman. That wouldn't be half as much fun."

He realized they had never talked about Sarah leaving him for Alice. They had been together long enough to make love several times, but they hadn't yet talked about what really mattered in their lives. But it was still early. They had plenty of time for that. She didn't plan to meet Rolf in Garberville for three more days, if she actually left. He had begun to believe that he could keep her here, that he might be able to steal her away from her guru.

"Sometimes I worry that I'm too aggressive with Rolfie," she continued. "I think he'd be happier, if we didn't make love so often. He'd never admit that, but I can tell. I love him a lot, but sometimes I think he gets tired of me. Our sex life is never as good as it is here with you."

Sasha smiled. He liked hearing this, but it gave him pause. He tried to imagine her living here with him or in her own place at Jeffrey's. He had fantasized endless times being with her, but it was always in sexual scenarios. He hadn't given much thought to what it would be like actually living together with her, in sickness and in health, as it were. He had always assumed she was permanently tied to Rolf, but increasingly he could imagine it differently. He treasured the space he had built for himself, the independence he had struggled so hard to create. But living alone was unnatural. He needed a woman. Was it her?

"We should walk down later to meet Meera," he heard himself say. He realized he had not responded to her comments about how good sex was with him. He pivoted back to that, but the delay was a little awkward. "I'm glad you like making love with me so much," he said. "It's fantastic for me. It's everything I've ever dreamed of. Our bodies seem to be made for each other. I love it." He could not say "you," not yet, anyway. That might come with time.

They spent more time in the garden. She asked him to teach her tai chi. He showed her where they got their water and they sat for a while by the buckeye tree he liked so much. In the late afternoon, they finally ventured down the path to Meera's cabin. He let go of her hand when they could see the house and Honey Lamb and the chickens. The Dutch door was half open but Meera wasn't inside. They walked around to her garden and found her there with an armful of pink, red and white hollyhocks. She turned to face them when she heard them approach.

"Those are beautiful," said Darlene. She looked around, "This garden is amazing."

"Meera, this is my friend Darlene," Sasha said. "Darlene, here is the master gardener herself, Miriam."

Meera took off one of her garden gloves and shook Darlene's hand and smiled. Sasha watched as they sized each other up. Meera was wearing some cutoff jeans, a pink tee shirt and her frayed wide-brimmed straw hat. There was sweat on her brow. She glanced at Darlene's hair that fell in two golden pigtails over her shoulders, at her belly ring and her white shorts and sandals. "I love your hair," said Meera. "You're very lucky."

"Thanks," said Darlene. "This is the most beautiful garden I've ever seen. You must work at it all the time."

"Thanks. It brings me a lot of joy and most of what I eat. The flowers are mostly perennials. They tend to behave themselves. Let's go inside. It's actually kind of muggy out here today. Would you like some tea?"

They turned and walked back to the cabin. "The weather is changing," noted Sasha. "We stopped to meet Kimmy and Bruce. They already started to harvest."

As they walked into Meera's cabin, Darlene's eyes opened wide, taking in every detail. "Did you really build this yourself?"

Meera laughed. "It shows, doesn't it? I'm not much for planning. I just put up one board after another. It kind of grew up on its own."

"I'm blown away. I couldn't imagine doing something like this. Where would you start?"

"Well, luckily for me, the chicken coop was already here, so I had two walls to work with. I mostly used whatever was available. It's a hodgepodge, but I love it."

Darlene kept turning and looking at everything with a look of wonder. Meera stoked the fire in the cook stove, lifted the triple ring hole and moved a kettle over it for tea. "Do you like Jasmine?" she asked.

"Thanks, yes, I'd love some," said Darlene.

They sat almost knee to knee by the bed. Meera rolled a joint and passed it to Darlene. "What's it like living here all by yourself?" asked Darlene. "I'm not sure I could do it."

Sasha sat quietly and watched. Darlene acted a little star struck, he thought, impressed with Meera's independence and self-confidence. Meera was Sasha's age, about eight years older than Darlene, and was the more experienced. He noticed how she kept turning the conversation back to Darlene. What had she enjoyed most on her trip around the world? How had that changed her? What had she learned in the ashram in India and, most particularly, what were her plans with Rolf?"

When Darlene mentioned how three of the girls in her community were pregnant, Meera asked, "Do you ever think of having children of your own?"

Darlene thought a moment before answering. "I guess I'm not sure. I know Rolfie doesn't want kids. He had a child with a woman in Germany and that didn't work out. I didn't think I'd ever want kids, but being around these friends who are pregnant made me question that. They were just like me before, not knowing what they wanted to do with their lives beyond the daily work in the commune. But now they're all super focused and, to be honest, I feel a little outside the circle. Their lives have real meaning and mine, well," she searched for the right words. "I kind of have to work at it all the time. Rolfie says it's just ego that wants to define our role in life. We should just accept whatever we do and do our best at it." She pointed around her. "I think you're living that."

"It takes a certain kind of person to live like this. I guess I'm a classic introvert. I like people, but most of all I like my solitude and my chickens," said Meera.

"And Honey Lamb," added Sasha.

"Ah, yes, I shouldn't forget Honey Lamb. She's getting a haircut tomorrow, thank God. You should come down and watch."

"What do you miss?" asked Darlene.

Meera thought before answering. "I miss sleeping with a man," she said at last.

Sasha was surprised to hear this and he was going to ask about her husband Tom, but stopped himself. Instead, he stood and said, "Thank you for the tea, Meer. We should give you back your solitude."

Meera stood and took the large bouquet of hollyhocks and handed them to Darlene. "Sasha's yurt could use a feminine touch. I've got bushels of these, as you saw."

"Thank you," said Darlene and embraced her warmly.

As they left to head up the path, she turned to Sasha and said, "Wow! What an amazing woman."

Chapter 34

She woke up, thinking she heard an owl. Owls were her totem animal. She was sure now the day would be propitious. She was supposed to meet Rolf in Garberville that afternoon. Sasha was still asleep facing the yurt wall. Darlene rolled off the bed onto all fours and crawled across the floor like a cat. She slipped on her sandals and walked out naked into the early morning light. There was a heavy dew on the ground.

She could not know the outcome of this day, but she had a premonition that whichever path she took, it would have consequences for years to come. She believed in fate, in pre-destination. She reassured herself that whatever was to come was for the best. Rolfie liked to say that "the film was already in the can." *Que será será.* Still, there were choices to be made. She didn't want to leave. She'd never felt as free as she did on Grizzly Mountain.

Making love with Sasha was divine. In releasing him from his inhibitions, she had given him the license he needed to discover his true self. Underneath all the academic pretensions was a natural lover, a sensualist. He took pleasure in pleasing a woman. They were wildly turned on to each other's bodies and he knew instinctively to move slowly, to bridle his passion, to tease her with forbearance. He allowed her own passion to reign; and often, just as she climaxed, he would come with her in a great roar. But, she noticed, that had not happened the last few times they made love. What had changed?

She opened the door to the chicken coop, but the hens were in no mood to get off their nests. She reached under them and extracted three eggs, taking care to leave the ones marked with an X. Then she went into the garden, grabbed the clippers hanging on the gate and gathered an enormous bouquet. When she entered the yurt, Sasha turned at the sound. "Where have you been?" he asked. "I missed you."

"I want to make you breakfast," she said. She stood naked before him, her arms full of flowers. She felt herself wet between her legs, but kept from moving to him. Instead, she walked to the sink, filled some jars with water and proceeded to light a fire in the cook stove. Sasha got out of bed and stretched. "It's going to be a lovely day," he said. He walked over to where she was cutting vegetables and put his arms around her, cupping her breasts. She turned her head and gazed into his eyes. He looked so content. Her own eyes were watery. She put down her knife and turned to face him and felt his dick harden against her.

"I don't know what to do, Sasha," she said, wiping away a tear. "I love it here." He knew what she meant. He understood that he could keep her here, steal her from Rolf, with just a word. He wanted to fuck her at that moment, but he hesitated. He didn't say anything. They kissed, but without passion. His silence cut through her. He could feel a terrible sense of loss in his gut. They held each other closely. Neither of them spoke.

She was determined to make love with him one last time before he drove her to town to meet Rolf. After breakfast, when the dishes were all done and put away and the flowers placed around the yurt, she said, "I'd like to make love with you in the shade under the pot plants. We can put a blanket down."

"We might get very sticky," said Sasha.

"With what?" she laughed.

He picked up a joint and a beach towel. He held out his hand and they walked together to the garden. The pot was frosted with resin that glittered in the sun. They were already naked. It felt like the Garden of Eden. He had his Eve, but still he hesitated. They smoked until they were too stoned to hold the joint. They made love with a deliberate patience. She had never felt herself wetter. He held back, waiting for her release. When she did, he did not come with her, but continued to slowly go in and out of her, ever deeper. He came with a sundering cry that rose from his tortured loins.

But she could sense a distance. She lay with her head on his chest and wished the moment could last forever. "How was that for you?" she asked.

"It was awesome. Thank you," he said. "And you?"

"It's always a peak experience with you, Sash. You are such a great lover."

"You taught me," he said.

She nodded. "You were a willing student. You seem far away today, though. What are you thinking about?"

"I'm just sad you're leaving," he lied. What he was really thinking had disturbed him, but he couldn't tell her. He had been thinking of Meera. Several times after they made love, he had thought of her when they finished. But the last few times he thought of her while they were still fucking, had fantasized about making love to Meera at the moment he came. He couldn't admit that to her. He was left feeling vulnerable and confused.

Suddenly, the whoosh whoosh sound of a motor rendered the air around them. It took a moment to register. "Helicopter!" said Sasha. "We need to get out of here." They jumped to their feet. He led her from the garden and hid against the back side of the chicken coop. Images of Vietnam rushed into his head, of hamlets burning, of helicopter assaults. He realized that clothes were their first line of defense, but they were in the yurt. He peeked around the corner and could see a man leaning out of one side with a telephoto lens. If they ran to the yurt, they'd get photographed, which could be used as evidence. The chopper flew right over the garden. When it passed, they rushed to the yurt.

"Shit, I never should have grown in the open like that. I don't think they're going to land, but they probably got a picture of Tuffy's license plate. We ought to get out of here," said Sasha.

The drive out the road and over the hill was filled with melancholy. Their parting was tinged with anxiety. "Well, they know what I've got now. That's for sure," said Sasha. "It might not be enough to trigger the expense of mounting a sheriff's raid. That was a National Forest helicopter. We're close to the border of Six Rivers National Forest. We're on private land, but they probably'll let the sheriff know what they found."

"Sasha," said Darlene. "I'm so sorry we had to end like this. This has been the best week of my life. I've loved every minute being here with you. It's perfect."

He didn't say anything. After a moment, she added, "I would have stayed, if you had asked me. But I know why you didn't."

He turned sharply to face her, "Why?' he said.

"Because you're in love with Meera." She smiled at him. "I understand. She's incredible."

It hit him like a blow. He had refused to let that thought into his brain. He felt a rush of adrenaline. He wanted to deny it to her, to ease her pain, but he couldn't. She was right, he realized. He pulled off the road and turned off the engine. The silence enveloped them. He looked at her, but couldn't think of what to say. Instead, he reached his arms around her and held her close for a long time. "Thank you, Darlene," he whispered at last. "You mean so much to me. Whatever happens, I want us to stay close."

She looked at him, eyes moist, and petted his face and his hair and kissed him on his forehead, his eyes and his lips. "Thank you, Sash. Come get me, if you change your mind."

They pulled off the Alderpoint Road and turned onto Garberville's main street. "Park here, please," she said. "I don't want you and Rolfie to have to meet." She grabbed her back pack, kissed him one last time and jumped out of Tuffy.

243

He watched her walk the block to the Wildflower Café, her blond braid trailing under her backpack behind her, watched her embrace a man dressed in a long shirt who was surprisingly shorter than she was. The man lifted her off the pavement. Sasha turned away, started Tuffy and headed back up the Alderpoint Road to Grizzly Mountain. He knew where he was going and what he had to do. He might lose his crop, or he might not. But he was coming home to Meera.

He had to wait close to his yurt for a small herd of cows meandering up the road, blocking his way. He was impatient. When he finally parked by the pond, he walked down the path to Meera's cabin. There was no smoke coming from her chimney, but when he looked inside, he saw Charles sitting in a chair smoking a joint. "Hey, bro," said Charles. "Did you see the chopper?"

"Yeah. It flew right over us in the garden," said Sasha.

"I wouldn't worry none," said Charles. "They was just looking. Forest Service guys."

"Where's Meer?" asked Sasha.

Charles laughed. Charles always laughed. "Her husband showed up, dressed all in white, a really cool dude with a beard down to here." He pointed to his waist. "The guy had some intense eyes. I liked him a lot. Rode a black Harley. You should have seen Meera riding out of here on the back of that chopper."

Sasha's heart stopped. The whole world seemed to stop. As if in a tunnel, he heard himself ask, "Did she say when they'd be back?"

"I dunno," said Charles.

Chapter 35

He struggled back up the path in a state of utter despair, his head swirling with anxiety. When he approached the yurt, he spotted cows in his lower garden, feasting on his weed. He ran up to them screaming and waving his arms. They were in no hurry to leave. He grabbed a shovel and whacked the lead one on her rump. He was furious, insane with anger and frustration. Finally, he managed to get them to move away from the garden and up past the madrone grove to higher ground. He chased them, yelling profanities, until they were far enough away from his crop. When he returned, drenched and spent, more cows had gathered in his garden.

He ran for help, but no one was around. Meera was somewhere with Tom. He didn't know where Bruce and Kimmy were. It was unlike them to be gone with their crop still in the ground. He yelled for Charles, but there was no response. He ran back to his lower garden, consumed with rage.

There are few things that focus the mind as sharply as standing face-to-face with a 1500-pound cow devouring your life's fortune. Sirens were screaming in Sasha's head—fire alarms of pain over Meera and Darlene—but the immediate threat from these bud-eating bovine beasts pushed those aside. This threat was happening in real time, inches away. With each passing second and each bite, Sasha's hard work and the bounty to live on were being devoured before his eyes.

"What the fuck!" Sasha said out loud. *I can't let this fucking happen,*" he said to himself. *To hell with animal rights.* He took a branch laying on the ground and struck it across the lead cow's face. No reaction. He threw dirt at it. He ran to the last cow in the back of the line and again whacked it hard, even lifted its tail and hit it. The cow kicked and moaned and finally pushed forward, rousting the others in the herd. They trotted off in a chorus of moos and turned up the road, in the opposite direction of the first herd. Sasha chased after them throwing rocks at their retreat. But, returning to the crime scene out of breath and drenched in sweat, he saw the other enemy squad had returned from their pasture. He knew somehow it was a losing battle, but he had no choice but to press on.

They came in tandem, one after another, as if they had carefully planned this larceny. Sasha tried everything he could think of. He fashioned a torch out of rags soaked in gasoline and waved the flames before their faces. They were undaunted. Their stoicism was heroic. His voice gone from screaming, Sasha grabbed an old saxophone he had been planning to learn to play and screeched and squealed into their ears to no effect. Finally, he took a bowling ball-sized rock and smashed it on the lead cow's brow, though without the force to kill it. The epoch battle went on for hours into the night, as he watched his crop get pummeled and chewed.

Sasha's arms were so tired, he could hardly lift the iron rake that was his weapon of choice. Seeing the end approaching, his mind turned to Meera and Darlene. In just over an hour, he reflected, he had lost the woman he now knew he loved and a lover who was passionate about him. And he was losing everything he had worked so hard for the last year, including all the plans and dreams that went with it. The pit at the bottom of his stomach had a trap door and he fell through it, flailing. The pain was so enormous, so without limits, it frightened him.

It was all his own fault, he told himself. He should have known long before that he had fallen in love with Meera. He kept denying it because of his petty fears. Had he professed himself to her, she might have embraced him. What had he to lose? He tried to convince himself that Meera felt the same as him. He could have stolen her from her inmate-husband, just as he knew he could have won Darlene. But he chose Meera. There really was no choice. He had already come to love her, even if he had not yet put words to it. He loved her grace, her exotic beauty, the way she walked, a certain elegance she had, the care and kindness she showed him, her indomitable self-reliance, and her groundedness. The thought of making love to her was almost too big to contemplate. Darlene had prepared him in the arts of love, but to love, to really and truly love another person, he would have Miriam.

But, Meera had departed on the back of her husband's Harley. He recounted Charles' description of the man, his intense eyes and long beard and how much Charles liked him. No doubt Meera did, too. Sasha had waited too long. He had missed his chance. He was sucker punched by his indecision. The thoughts that had filled his head on the ride back from Garberville of a life in this paradise with Meera floated away like so much smoke. All he could do now was fight with whatever energy he had left to save his crop.

The smell of cows nauseated him. He considered killing one of them, but they belonged to the judge who would not appreciate that, he knew. Besides, he had not the heart for it. He did what he was capable of for as long as he could. In the end, the cows wouldn't budge no matter what form of torture he employed. Stoned they were. He had battled them straight through the night. Daylight was breaking at last. He let go his rake and plopped on the ground as he watched the cows finish off the last leaf.

At last he stood up, turned his back on the victorious cows and walked through the madrone grove, up past his grieving tree to the buckeye tree where he hoped someday to be buried. As he climbed ever higher, he became more convinced of his love for Meera, fueling his grief. He recalled how she fed and cared for him when his back was out, how she patiently taught him how to sprout seeds, sex his plants and grow his crop. Now all that was ruined. He thought of her holding Jeffrey's body in her arms, crying. He pictured all the times she brought him cake and pies, how she turned him onto *Dune*, had given him the framed passage from it that now hung by his door, and he remembered their acid trip together when he had wanted to kiss her. If only they had. But he was too weak, too passive.

The pain of loss was unbearable. He felt like vomiting. His head was about to explode. He was such a wimp, too weak to chase away a few cows. Surely, Charles or Bruce would have known what to do. He just wasn't cut out for this life. He had given it his all, but it wasn't enough. He was still the professor, a useless intellectual, a phony. He had failed and the realization of his failure burned more than his loss of love or income. He began to cry. Reaching the outcrop of rocks around the buckeye tree, Sasha sat down and poured out his soul, sobbing uncontrollably.

Listening to himself cry, something suddenly gave way. He looked up as the sun lit the top of the trees and the hills that cascaded below him. He pictured Jeffrey laughing at him and, in a flash of insight, he got the joke. What he was experiencing as tragedy, was actually very funny: a bunch of stoned cows had eaten his crop. He could hear Jeffrey's voice. "Look around you, Sash. How are things right now?" In the blinding light of reality, he realized he was, in fact, sitting in paradise. He was strong and healthy, not weak and pathetic. He had learned to live by himself, to grow his own food, to be self-sufficient. He lived naked half the day, swam in rivers, chopped his wood, ran across the hills on hardened bare feet like an animal.

He stood up and looked at the immense beauty around him. There were no other dwellings to see. Off in the distance, there was a large herd of deer grazing on wild grasses. The only sound was of the wind blowing through the trees. Below him, he saw some cows meandering aimlessly and he started to laugh and then his laughter grew and grew and couldn't be contained. The tears he shed now were tears of joy. He experienced redemption and a full appreciation of his freedom. He may have lost his crop and his love, but he was free.

In the distance he heard the grinding pop-pop, potato-potato cadence of a Harley approaching. It was probably Meera returning with Tom. Life would go on.

Sasha started to walk back down the mountain, his feet gripping the earth with confidence. He smiled as he walked. He felt unburdened. There were still plants to harvest in the fenced garden, half eaten by grasshoppers, but enough to get him through another year. He would survive, though there'd be no trips to Thailand or Mexico this winter. Again, he heard the Harley, but it was driving away and caught a glimpse of Tom, by himself.

Sasha walked by his fenced garden that was coming to life in the dawn light. He felt lighter than he had ever felt before, in a kind of wonder, in full awareness of everything around him. Again, he could hear Jeffrey telling him, "Live without hope or fear. The future doesn't exist. Only the present is real." As he approached the yurt, he saw Lady Jessica and Caliber sitting together by the front door.

Acknowledgement

Editors are the unsung heroes of literature. If you read a work of fiction and can't stop turning the pages, you can bet that it was well edited by someone other than the author. I got my first taste of the editor's scalpel when my editor, Jane Rogers, cut out 10,000 words from my debut book, *Citizens Rising: Independent Journalism and the Spread of Democracy* (CUNY Journalism Press 2013), a non-fiction account of the role of media activists in recent history. I remember lying in a fetal position on the floor crying at the loss of what Stephen King calls the "little darlings." We writers get real attached to our progeny. In my most recent novel, Jane had me remove seven chapters. Ouch! But one gets used to it when we realize how much stronger the book becomes. It takes someone of great strength of character to speak truth to authors and an exquisite ear. Jane Rogers has both of these in surplus. But it is not only the art of excision. As my editor, she also contributed significantly to plot and character development. I feel the most profound debt of gratitude to Jane, who is in every sense of the word my partner. If my books have any value, a lot of the credit must go to her.

www.ingramcontent.com/pod-product-compliance
Lightning Source LLC
Chambersburg PA
CBHW021006120726
47905CB00009B/2884

* 9 7 8 0 9 9 9 7 6 4 5 4 1 *